The Eighth Wonder of the World

Jordan Plevnes

Translated from the Macedonian by Will Firth

Plamen
Press

Washington, DC

Plamen Press

9039 Sligo Creek Pkwy Suite 1114 Silver Spring, Maryland 20901

www. plamenpress.com

Copyright © Jordan Plevnes, 2019

Published by Plamen Press, 2019

Printed in the United States of America

10 9 8 7 6 5 4 3 2 1

PUBLISHER'S CATALOGING-IN-PUBLICATION DATA

Names: Plevnes, Jordan, author. | Firth, Will, translator.
Title: The Eighth Wonder of the World / Jordan Plevnes ; [translated by] Will Firth.
Description: Silver Spring, MD : Plamen Press, 2019.

Identifiers: ISBN 978-0-9960722-6-7 (paperback)
LCCN 2019949965 (print)

Subjects: LCSH: Macedonian fiction--Translations into English.
Berlin Wall, Berlin, Germany, 1961-1989--Fiction.
Balkan Peninsula--History--Fiction. | Satire. | Black humor.
BISAC: FICTION / Satire. | FICTION / Humorous / Black Humor.
FICTION / Absurdist.

Classification: LCC PG1196.26.L4813 E43 2019 (print)
LCC PG1196.26.L4813 (ebook)   DDC 891.8/19--dc23.

Translated from the Macedonian by Will Firth
Cover Design by Roman Kostovski

Editors

Rachel Miranda Feingold

Roman Kostovski

Foreword

On the International Recognition
of Jordan Plevnes's Work

Macedonian author, playwright, and poet, Jordan Plevnes emerged for the first time on the American cultural scene a year before the fall of the Berlin Wall, with the performance of his landmark play *R.*, about which leading theatrologist Robert W. Corrigan stated: "After only 5 minutes of watching *R*, I knew that Plevnes's plays would be performed in the international theater repertoire."

Undoubtedly there is more than one reason why Jordan Plevnes has received international recognition for his contribution to world literature. Since the curtain opened on his first play, *Erigon*, in 1982 up until his most recent drama, *The Eternal House*, his plays have been performed in Macedonian, European, and U.S. theatres over a span of 35 years, bringing powerful and captivating images that unify his playwriting style with themes such as nationalism, revolution, rebellion, idealism, and anarchy.

Since 1988, three plays by Plevnes have been performed on American stages: *R, The Fall of Albert Camus* and *Happiness is a New Idea in Europe,* which received favorable recognition from *The New York Times.* When one considers his work as a whole — translated and performed in multiple languages throughout the world— the publication of his novel *The Eighth Wonder of the World* in Washington DC, on the occasion of the 30th anniversary of the fall of the Berlin Wall, has a somewhat symbolic meaning, bringing his craft to a full circle.

In his fiction, Plevnes continuously returns to his original analysis—the historical paradoxes of the European idea, suggesting that, instead of a *Europeanisation of the Balkans*, we have a *Balkanisation of Europe.* For Plevnes, the small countries and nations of the Old Continent will probably remain the only defenders of European idealism. He explores whether Macedonia and the Balkans uniquely identify themselves on their own terms, or if they are identified by clichés such as "a crossroad of dead empires" or "a crossroad of dialogue among civilizations."

Plevnes is a contemporary sociologist in an age of degradation and destruction. He is a gifted writer who breaks borders and embodies hope and faith in the future of the world we live in. Moreover, through the prism of Macedonia, he builds relations, encouraging a climate of open dialogue among civilizations. For

Plevnes, both Macedonian and European aspirations reveal an everlasting and inevitable struggle in two opposite directions— survival or death, analogous to the two known relations of man's existence, birth, and death.

His work entices us because it captures an unlimited and creative human freedom of expression. Since *Erigon*, Plevnes has demolished the prevailing canons of traditional Macedonian drama. Through the composition of his characters and construction of fluid events and locations, Plevnes injects the impulsive, spontaneous, improvised, emotional, and imaginative—creating associative, mythic, and poetic images. He treats religious and cultural differences as global issues with both blatant and subtle irony, or as Professor Hedy Bouraoui from York University in Toronto so adequately expressed, "sometimes with a piercing irony in terms of the colossal absurdities of the world we live in today."

In its entirety, the work of Jordan Plevnes sends a universal message about the meaning of ideas, dreams, hope, and humanism—of the immortality of beauty, of the possibility of the impossible, and of the transient as eternal. He believes an idea cannot be called an idea if it's not a dangerous one. And his credo is boldly emphasized in this novel, *The Eighth Wonder of the World*.

In June of 2006, during a symposium at the Sorbonne in Paris dedicated to Plevnes's work, *Publishers Weekly* European correspondent Herbert Lottman called the Macedonian writer "a magician who can unite and formulate an eternity of beauty with the tragic images of world history."

The Eighth Wonder of the World is yet another of Jordan Plevnes's parables of hope. His preoccupation with the role of beauty in the context of social, religious, and cultural differences recurs here, and the question is posed: Does humanism have a prospect of survival in the future of humankind? Again, he posits that survival and idealism can still be found in beauty and art—and that only beauty and art have the power to save the world.

THE EIGHTH WONDER
OF THE WORLD

For Liljana, Konstantin, and Ilija

A heavy gypsy with an untamed beard and sparrow hands, who introduced himself as Melquíades, put on a bold public demonstration of what he himself called the eighth wonder of the learned alchemists of Macedonia.

Gabriel García Márquez, *One Hundred Years of Solitude*

The hatred which divides nation from nation, race from race, class from class,
Father, forgive.
The covetous desires of people and nations to possess what is not their own,
Father, forgive.
The greed which exploits the work of human hands and lays waste the earth,
Father, forgive.
Our envy of the welfare and happiness of others,
Father, forgive.
Our indifference to the plight of the imprisoned, the homeless, the refugee,
Father, forgive.
The lust which dishonors the bodies of men, women and children,
Father, forgive.
The pride which leads us to trust in ourselves and not in God,
Father, forgive.

The Coventry Litany of Reconciliation

Apart from his first name and the fact that his father was called Philip, Alexander Simsar had nothing in common with Alexander the Great. The conqueror seized all of the known world and died at the age of thirty-three. Alexander Simsar lived in vain and lost his life in 3.3 seconds.

I will tell you his story . . .

1.0 Seconds

As an eleven-year-old, on the day of his father's burial in the Macedonian village of V., Alexander Simsar fell asleep in front of the open grave to the words of the chanting priest: "For the Lord Himself will descend from heaven with a shout, with the voice of an archangel, and with the trumpet of God. And the dead in Christ will rise first. Then we who are alive and remain shall be caught up together with those in the clouds to meet the Lord in the air . . ."

Those last words that he heard, "to meet the Lord in the air," whisked him away into a deep, childish dream and he overslept the rest of the funeral. He slept soundly, sitting on the stone perimeter of the family tomb, despite his mother's tears raining down on his face and despite the earsplitting lamentations of the five old women clad in black who were said to be the last professional mourners in Europe—the only remnant of ancient tragedy in modern-day Macedonia.

Imagine: he dreamed he was holding the nearby Lake Ohrid in his hands, which together with Lake Baikal in southern Siberia and Lake Tanganyika in equatorial Africa is one of the three oldest lakes in the world—scientists estimate it to be about 150 million years old. He dreamed he was holding the lake in his hands and that it spoke to him and looked into his sleeping child's eyes: "Listen to me, I am 150 million years old and I know what I'm saying! You are the descendant of a family of masons, one of the oldest in the Balkans. For centuries your ancestors built houses and temples, castles and bridges, palaces and wondrous buildings of every kind, from the Urals to the Atlantic. I remember every single one, and they all came to rinse their eyes in my water. For I was the secret mirror that saw in their faces the despair of the remote places they returned from, and at the same time I recognized their implacable determination not to be chained to their birthplace. Mark my words, Alexander Simsar! Your family tree is one of facade artists who carried out the most demanding stone carvings on the tallest buildings, from here almost to the end of the world. Remember that, Alexander Simsar, on the day of the death of your father, Philip. Make a vow, pluck a wish from your little heart, and imagine an eternal structure you will give to this world, my mortal, sleeping child, because there is nothing else in this false world but sun, water, and stone. Before you reach the sun, you will burn; before you make it to the water, it will carry you away; your only chance is stone—you will either leave your name in it, like on a grave, or turn its stony silence into a thought that lives eternally!"

Thus spoke Lake Ohrid to the child, Alexander, and returned to where it had lain for around 150 million years. Alexander awoke and saw a sprig of basil in his folded, clenched hands; it was wet with his mother's tears. He also saw the gravediggers leveling the mound on his father's grave. Spring was in full bloom. Petals of plum, cherry, and apple trees blew onto the soil that covered his father's coffin, and even his soul seemed to have turned to fruit blossom, which made Alexander think that he himself was descended from fruit!

The funeral ended and the mourners walked to the churchyard to honor the soul of the deceased with a meal of white beans and red fish. Before they went home, his mother kissed the wooden cross, and he laid the basil on his father's fresh grave.

On the way he told his mother about the dream.

"It reminds me of your birth," she said. "Your father was away. It was God's will that you should come into the world in the Dimovskis' water mill, where I had gone to grind some grain. Old Pauna Dimovska put you on the iron scales that are otherwise used for flour for the hungry mouths of V. She weighed you, and I can still hear her words as if it was yesterday: 'The child has a star on its forehead; it will see the world as far as it goes, and the world will see it.' What the lake told you, Alexander, is true. God protect you and show you the way to that great dream!"

But you don't have to imagine anything, dear reader,

because his fate has already decided everything.

How did that happen? It was quite simple: that sublime dream left its imprint on the whole life of Alexander Simsar, who as an adult was nicknamed "the Great" because of his height of six feet four. He weighed ten-and-a-half stone, a weight that did not change from his twentieth birthday until now, at the age of fifty. His personal tragedy was that he took the dream of Lake Ohrid literally, and that, literally, cost him his life.

The chronological cornerstones of his life, which he lived in the twentieth century, were as follows. He was born in 1939. His father, Philip Simsar, died in 1950 at the age of thirty-seven when he leaped from a window of Idrizovo Prison in Skopje; as a fighter for the autonomy of Macedonia, which at the time was part of Yugoslavia, he had been sentenced to life imprisonment by the Macedonian Communists.

Alexander was left alone with his mother, Stoyanka. He attended classical lyceum in Bitola and then studied architecture at the University of Skopje. In 1967, he married the beautiful, blonde Tsveta Mikhailova from his native village, who broke off her education at medical school in Bitola due to the intensity of her feelings for him, although she was not yet eighteen. His father's death weighed heavily on Alexander's mind, and, since he found no work in his own country, he went to West Germany in 1969—one of the first postwar Macedonian architects to leave his homeland.

His first destination was Hamburg, the gateway to Europe, where he diligently studied German, found temporary work, and tried to gain the attention of architectural firms and design agencies with a German translation of his university degree from Skopje. He soon realized there was no chance of it being recognized in Germany even in theory, let alone in practice. After reading a job advertisement for a facade restoration artist with the West Berlin firm World Construction LLC, he applied, was taken on, and remained with the firm for twenty years. During all that time he returned to Macedonia once a year during the winter months to visit Tsveta—the couple had no children—and his mother, who later died in his absence.

For twenty years he practiced one of the most difficult crafts in the world. For twenty years his shadow flitted against the facades of tall buildings in Europe, America, South Asia, the Middle and Far East, and for twenty years he was pursued by the dream he had dreamed at his father's funeral, with Lake Ohrid in his hands and the question of what he should build from stone and how he could leave an immortal trace in the world during his mortal life.

He got so used to heights that he felt like he was walking in the sky even when walking on the ground; and conversely, when he was very close to the clouds, he sensed the smell of the earth. At any rate, visions of that structure were only revealed to him on days when he saw the infinite blue of the heavens. When it clouded over, when the days were dark, whatever the latitude, he thought only of his earthly responsibilities. One of the most important of these was to build up savings in his Deutsche Bank account; his monthly earnings sometimes reached 10,000 deutschmarks and grew in direct proportion to the many ideas for the stone structure, five of which were shortlisted in his mind.

The first idea was to build an All-Balkan Church of Love, where the many different peoples of the Balkans could come and pray as equals, but he had three major reservations about this idea. First, he could not decide on a specific location, because many architects before him had died with the realization that nothing was built in the Balkans where it should have been. Second, he was unsure about the term "church" and did not want non-Christians or Jews to think that the church should negate mosques and synagogues. This second reservation was reinforced by his own modest experiences, which told him that love in the Balkans was an impossibility, as suggested by the proverb: "When two make love in the Balkans, they usually do it over the dead body of another." And third, he shared the thought of the American journalist Sulzberger, who noted in his descriptions of the Balkan Peninsula: "The peoples of the Balkans have two common features: they eat spicy food and have a propensity to kill each other!"

The second idea was to build a transparent stone construction, The Death of Europe, which would display objects of famous personalities, artifacts, and the written testimony of a civilization that had been moving at the speed of a turtle for more than 2,000 years, producing only the evidence of its sluggish continuity and impending death. But two sensitive issues stood in the way of this idea: its necrophilia, and the divergent stages of disintegration in East and West.

The third idea was even more morbid and thus virtually

unrealizable: a tower of human bones named The Crimes of the Twentieth Century.

The fourth idea was closest to his heart but called for great preparation: an International House of Global Poverty to be set up in New York, with offices in Paris, Berlin, London, Tokyo, Rio de Janeiro, Johannesburg, New Delhi, and Moscow. As an architect who had dreamed fruitlessly for twenty years, confronted with the fact that the history of world architecture is the history of wealth, he was convinced that the construction of these nine stone structures in the form of phalluses penetrating the sky, each based on a vaginal pedestal, would allow the history of global poverty to be depicted: the transformation of human beings from monkey to beast, leaving millions of people destitute, starving, and naked, with only the inherited and unlimited right to go down on each other, but without any guarantee of survival. That would be a real hit in the world of architecture, in his opinion—an immortalization of the culture of poverty!

The fifth idea was a Museum of Political Lies from Antiquity to the Present, but he didn't know which country in the world would allow him to realize the project. Besides, the idea seemed too general to him, because life itself could be regarded as a plain lie.

Alexander Simsar, nicknamed "the Great," kept absolutely mum about his ideas. He did not confide them to anyone, except once. In the winter of 1988, he came to V. during Carnival, when almost all the inhabitants wore different costumes and masks of animals, angels, monsters, and ghosts, transforming the village into a colorful one-day mystery, and awakening the pagan winds of lost centuries of memory near the 150 million-year-old lake.

That day, his wife Tsveta told him the advice of a well-known Romany clairvoyant who had come all the way from India with a group of traveling tinsmiths: to become pregnant, her husband had to make love to her at midnight by the wave-battered eastern wall of the Kalishta Monastery church on the shore of the lake. The lake would give strength to the seed, and God would bless them with offspring.

After Carnival that same evening, shortly before midnight, they went down to Kalishta together, to the east side of the church, and as the waves of the lake pounded at Tsveta's hair, eyes, lips, and breasts, Alexander drove into her again and again with such force that the crosses trembled on the graves of the nuns at the other end of the monastery.

In the moment before his climaxe, instead of devoting himself fully to his beloved wife, his gaze was drawn to the lake, and with horror he saw the same picture from his childhood dream and heard the terrible words that came from the mouth of the lake:

"Alexander Simsar! Soon it will be forty years since I spoke to you about the eternal structure. How much longer are you going to wait? Your days are numbered and death may be lurking around the next corner. You must make your decision and begin to build!"

The mouth of the lake closed and he looked again at Tsveta, who stood before him against the eastern wall of the church as if crucified and naked; the waves of the lake overflowed their lips and their bodies, which now writhed in a cry of perfection, as if he himself was the lake and she herself the church, in whom the long-awaited God-child of their tormented hearts should be conceived.

That winter night was wonderful, as if all the hidden warmth of the Mediterranean watched over the Ohrid Riviera. On the way back to V. through the reeds and willow groves, Tsveta's hair waved before him like a bright flag, a reflection of the January moon, and when they arrived at the threshold of their house he entrusted himself to her:

"I have a premonition that our child was conceived this night! I also feel I'm nearing the realization of my life's dream of an eternal structure I will commit to world history." And he told her about his five most vivid ideas.

But not everything was as it should have been. He returned to Berlin and continued his daily work for World Construction. The news from Tsveta was rather depressing, and his indecision regarding his childhood dream entered a dramatic phase—he felt he was losing the ground under his feet and the sky under his hands.

What happened next came like a bolt out of the blue.

The idea of the eternal structure hit him, or fell from the sky over Berlin, on September 21, 1989 at precisely 12:53 p.m. Central European Time.

Why exactly at that moment? A few months before, as he breathed the air of divided West and East Berlin, he had felt a huge, invisible key opening the Brandenburg Gate; he sensed an unknown wind, perhaps from Moscow or Washington, which would blow down the Berlin Wall; with his own eyes from high above, he saw the Iron Curtain of the ideologically divided world open; he perceived that a great mingling of the free and unfree peoples was imminent, teeming through the empty space of a new age; Communism, which had held almost half of the planet in its power, would wither and fall within the next twenty-four hours at most.

On the night of September 20–21, he had a strange dream. He saw the familiar picture from his childhood, in front of the open grave, into which the wooden coffin with the lifeless body of his father was to be lowered. Suddenly the coffin opened and turned into an astounding stone structure in the shape of a cradle; it began to rock, and his father, who had suddenly become a one-year-old child, spoke to him: "My son Alexander, you shall erect a building in our home village in Macedonia that does not exist anywhere else in the world, because no one has thought of inventing it. You shall call it 'The Cradle of the World,' because the cradle and the coffin are the same everywhere, in all religions and all languages. Only birth and death are always the same everywhere!"

At these words, Alexander Simsar "the Great" awoke and felt a terrible thirst. He switched on the light in the studio apartment in Kreuzberg, went into the kitchen in his pajamas, and drank a tall glass of water. At the bottom of the empty glass he thought he saw the lake from his childhood dream, but he had drained it of water. After that, he could not go back to sleep.

On September 21, 1989, at exactly 9 a.m., Alexander started work near the top of the damaged spire of the Berlin Kaiser Wilhelm Memorial Church, where the World Construction firm was carrying out a restoration project. He had to chisel out fine details like the wings of birds, children's heads, the eyes of angels, or heavenly fruit. From nine until twelve he worked without interruption and thought about almost nothing at all. At twelve o'clock he went down the scaffolding with the plan to have a small snack and then continue. But he could barely open his mouth. He only drank a glass of water, and in it he saw his father's face. He climbed back up the damaged steeple, marveling at the Memorial Church in its ruined glory from top to bottom, and, in a thrill of exaltation that ran through his body, forgot to fasten his protective harness. At the same time, he dropped his chisel and it fell down and landed on the sidewalk of Kurfürstendamm Avenue, and when he looked down after it he felt as if he himself was falling, featherlike, down toward the paved sidewalk. As he floated down, he saw before his eyes the stone structure called the Cradle of the World, which he was to build with a child's head on the top; he saw all his past life and also his future life, saw the earth and himself lying in it, while a choir of angels with children's faces sang a lullaby to him, which was also a song of mourning.

An ambulance and the World Construction rescue team arrived at 12:59 p.m. exactly. Alexander lay prostrate on the ground in his white overalls, unconscious, his eyes open and staring at the sky. He was rushed from the Memorial Church to Berlin's Augusta Victoria Hospital and just seventeen minutes later, admitted to the neurosurgical department headed by Professor Rudolf Benn.

At 3 p.m. that same afternoon, Hans Neubauer, Deputy Manager of World Construction LLC, arrived on the earliest possible flight from Frankfurt. He was received by Professor Benn, who informed him that Mr. Simsar had gradually regained consciousness one hour after being admitted to the hospital. He was out of danger; his left knee and right shoulder fractures would heal quickly. The CT scan showed a minor injury to his cerebral orientation center, but there was no need for surgery. At most, it could manifest itself later in certain inverse movements when performing everyday activities, for example the patient could go right instead of left, look down instead of up, think a great spatial distance was a small one (2,000 miles could seem like two miles), or see infinity instead of the finiteness of life . . . And one more detail: a slight injury to this part of the cerebrum causes a surge in hormonal activity that stimulates the affected person's sexual life and heightens their fantasies to the extreme.

Just then, Hans Neubauer burst out laughing and hugged Professor Benn heartily.

"I think you understand my excitement, Professor Benn. I'm so happy that one of our best facade artists has become a medical phenomenon! To fall from such a great height and stay alive without serious consequences—it's simply a miracle . . . I've not come across any other example in my long civil engineering career. Please allow me to express my deepest gratitude on behalf of World Construction LLC, and also personally."

Finally, Professor Benn informed him that the patient's friends and family could come to visit in three days' time. He would have to stay in the hospital for about fifteen days.

During the first three days, Alexander Simsar "the Great" felt as if he was weightless. Whether he was in bed or he got up to go to the bathroom, he felt like he was flying. Already on the day after the fall, he refused with the utmost respect and kindness the food that the nurse brought to the table in his room. Professor Benn then went in to see him with an almost reproachful tone, but the phenomenal patient answered with impeccable calm:

"Professor Benn, let me tell you my personal and professional secret. I've been working as a facade artist for twenty years and only eat selected food: Chasselas grapes, boiled spinach, acacia honey, dried peppers, if possible from southeastern Europe—cooked, peeled, and braised with leek—curdled sheep's milk, and some common types of fruit: cherries, pears, apples, and peaches. That's all. No meat! The only fish I eat is Ohrid trout, but it's a rarity in the freshwater world of Macedonia!"

"Does that mean you come from the land of Alexander, the greatest emperor of all time?"

"Yes . . . I also happen to bear his name," the fallen patient said, slightly surprised, and added: "But there are also serious historians who call him a 'jester and bandit on a grand scale.'"

"I have to tell you that I'm impressed by your case!" Professor Benn continued. "Perhaps it's no coincidence that you bear the name of the youngest and undeniably most energetic emperor in the world, no matter how many pass judgement on him. Besides, millions of people from different nations have the same name. But perhaps your fall in Berlin is your own personal conquest of the world. I haven't heard of a comparable example in the history of falls anywhere in the world!"

At that point Professor Benn was called to an urgent operation and Alexander remained alone in his room, with a feeling of immense happiness.

"Dear Professor Benn, may God give you health and fulfill all your wishes. By attaching international importance to my fall, you also give credence to the plan I will later implement," he said aloud.

On the seventh day, his World Construction workmates informed him that his wife Tsveta would be arriving on October 1 at 9 a.m. This would be her fourth proper visit to Berlin, not counting the three previous trips, which were for medical examinations to do with their unfulfilled desire for children. They had tried all the latest methods, including in vitro fertilization, but nothing seemed to help. The last time, in the fall of 1984, they consulted one of West Berlin's best specialists, Dr. Blumenthal.

"You know, state-of-the-art medicine cannot help you," he told the Simsars. "The problem is that nothing is really wrong! On the male side we have megalospermia, which means that instead of 20–200 million sperm per milliliter, the normal range, there are 400 million; on the female side we have a very rare condition called *Vulvitis carpe diem*, where the sperm are burned before they can fulfill their fertilizing function. My conclusion: paramedical experience shows that there are options and positions that can lead to a solution in such cases, but that will depend on the magic of the moment, which you have to find yourselves. I have no doubts as to your erotic imagination. Good luck, and may God be with you!"

Five whole years had passed since then. Alexander awaited his wife in the same childless state, although they had tried various paramedical means, the most recent of which was having sex at midnight by the eastern wall of the church by the lake—still without the desired result.

With this thought and in his weightless condition, Alexander awaited Tsveta.

The door of the hospital room opened and Tsveta stood there petrified, her eyes glowing as she looked at him.

"My angel," she sighed.

"Forgive me," he said.

"Why?"

He did not answer.

"When they called me and said you'd fallen from a great height," Tsveta went on, "I gathered all the churches of Macedonia in my heart, shaped it into a candle, and lit it for you, to burn for your health."

She cried. He didn't.

"How is . . . Macedonia?" Alexander asked.

"Something's seething in the Balkans. I don't know what's coming."

"Something's seething in Europe and all around the world," he reflected.

"Maybe they'll finish Macedonia off," she said bleakly.

They fell silent.

"As I was falling, I thought I was going to free Macedonia," he told her after a while.

"Free it? From whom?"

"From me."

"And then?" she asked.

"And then . . . nothing. When I saw I'd survived, I said to myself: I'm going to do the reverse."

"What?"

"I'm going to free myself of the Macedonia in me," he explained.

"What does that mean?"

"I dreamed that with God's help I'd build a stone structure in Macedonia, on a peak of the Galichitsa Range, where you can look down at Lake Ohrid and Lake Prespa. The building will be called the Cradle of the World. Every stone will have the dimensions of a newborn baby and a name of its own— the names of the Savior Children and the Murderer Children in world history—since all humans, both the creators of beauty and humanity's monsters, are sired by a father and borne by a mother."

Her eyes pierced him with the thought of their common, unborn child. He began to kiss her tears and then drink them as they rolled over her face.

"And I'll be together with you and the child we'll have," he consoled her.

So ended their first reunion in the Augusta Victoria Hospital.

On the fifteenth day, Professor Benn came into Alexander's room smiling from ear to ear, and read him the contents of the medical report. It said that, after surviving the fall, the patient was certified unfit for work for three months. Five medical checkups would be carried out in that period, and the results would determine what further treatment might be required.

Tsveta decided to stay on with Alexander in Berlin, so they spent the three months in his apartment in Kreuzberg. He had no obligations except for the checkups, which he went to as planned. During that time, he was witness to the true historical basis for his idea, growing ever more confident in it as he watched the epoch-making developments on TV, and also traced the evolution of the designs for the Cradle of the World that buzzed around in his sick, concussed head.

It was autumn, and as he lay motionless in bed, the movements of history unfolded before him. He saw the demolition of the great monuments of Lenin, Stalin, and a gamut of other communist rulers who had ruled over half the planet. He saw the fall of the Berlin Wall and also collected three small pieces of concrete in the immediate vicinity of the place where the famous Russian dissident and cellist Mstislav Rostropovich gave his celebrated spontaneous concert in honor of the event. He saw the beginnings of the collapse of the Soviet Union and Yugoslavia. He followed the live broadcast of the execution of the Romanian dictator Ceauşescu and his wife. The Central Committee headquarters of the Bulgarian Communist Party in Sofia went up in flames, and in Albania an emaciated man shat on Enver Hoxha's head. He saw Prague and Budapest, and Warsaw in particular, liberated from the heads, bodies, and dead souls that disappeared in the black smoke of historical delusions. An inner fire burned in his jolted head—he had the feeling that he had fallen at just the right time to complete the building he imagined.

At the end of December 1989, after the fifth checkup, the specialists of the Augusta Victoria Hospital issued him a report certifying that he was permanently unfit for facade work after his fall. His twenty years' service meant that he was entitled to a lifelong pension from Germany amounting to 2,936 deutschmarks.

That same evening, Hans Neubauer, Deputy Manager of World Construction LLC, gave a festive dinner in honor of Alexander Simsar, nicknamed "the Great," and his wife Tsveta in the Goethe's Garden restaurant overlooking the Spree River. This subtly emotional event was also attended by a dozen workmates of our selfless facade artist. When the time came for his thank-you toast, Alexander raised his glass, took a tiny piece of concrete from the Berlin Wall out of his pocket, and proceeded to smash it with a small hammer. He picked up the dust with his right hand, let it trickle into his wineglass, and spoke:

"I raise this glass to the countless heights I have scaled, thanks to World Construction. Dear colleagues and management, I wish you all a long and happy life! I drink this wine with a pulverized piece of the Berlin Wall so it may course through my bloodstream to highlight the solemn moment of its fall—and my own—at this time where the paths of freedom and rapprochement between East and West are opening up in our common European home. This is the salvation for small European nations like the remnant of my small country, Macedonia. Twice in the twentieth century, the horrors of human evil were unleashed in Germany in the form of the two world wars. This time, may the beauty of hope and salvation emanate from Germany and spread to Europe and the whole world! As a modest contribution, I will build a stone structure in Macedonia, unique in world history, which will combine two key experiences of my life: the childhood dream during the funeral of my father and the moment of my fall, when I saw exactly, down to the last tenth of an inch, how this remarkable building is going to look, which you could call the Eighth Wonder of the World . . ."

At that point, an awkward pause ensued. Alexander's World Construction workmates looked at him with a mixture of enthusiasm and compassion. He perceived his great verve to be quite normal, and after the fall it was enhanced by prodigious self-confidence: he talked about what he intended to do as if it was already done, no more, no less! With his glass in his raised hand, his jolted mind flagged . . . He just stood there, dressed for the festive occasion in a black suit and a white shirt, hand-embroidered by his mother, buttoned up to the top. Tsveta had brought it with her, to dress her husband in for the trip back to Macedonia—God forbid, dead, or, God willing, alive. His arm was still raised, holding the glass, but his mind faltered and his mouth froze . . .

Tsveta paled in fear on the chair to his right.

"God almighty!" she exclaimed to herself. "Have you ever seen a dead man standing upright on both legs, with his arm raised?"

And then?

As if nothing had happened, he opened his mouth again, moistened his lips briefly with his tongue, and continued:

"You were perhaps surprised when I spoke of an eighth wonder of the world. *We know there are seven wonders of the world*, you probably said. But hardly anyone knows them all, and who can name them all by heart? Before I drink this glass to commemorate the fall of the Berlin Wall and my own fall—and drink to your well-being and in honor of my dear Tsveta, who has come from Macedonia to take me home alive or dead—I'll remind you of the Seven Wonders of the World as described by Philo in his work *De septem orbis miraculis* toward the end of the third century, BC. After that I'll tell you about the eighth.

"First, Philo mentions the Pyramid of Cheops in Egypt. Second, the Hanging Gardens of Semiramis in Babylon. Third, Phidias's statue of Zeus at Olympia, made of gold and ivory. Fourth, the Temple of Artemis at Ephesus. Fifth, the Mausoleum at Halicarnassus. Sixth, the Colossus of Rhodes, a statue of the sun god Helios. And seventh, the Lighthouse of Alexandria. But what is the eighth? That is the secret I wish to share with you: the Cradle of the World in Macedonia!

"I'll build this Eighth Wonder of the World atop the

Galichitsa Range in Macedonia, which has a direct view of Lake Ohrid and Lake Prespa. This is one of the most beautiful landscapes not only in Europe, but in the whole world, at least as far as I personally have seen. Yes, Europe needs such a new wonder of the world to overcome the historical logic of its existence, which is marked by a huge machine of death by the two dominant ideologies of the twentieth century, fascism and communism. Earlier, in the nineteenth century, a famous Russian novel termed Europe 'the world's most expensive grave' because of its mercantilism, which, in the new conditions after the fall of the Berlin Wall and the lifting of the Iron Curtain, threatens to enslave people once more in the shackles of consumption and make them forget they're only guests in this world. Consciously or not, they are to become slaves to the ideology that has held its own for several centuries: the ideology of capitalism, and the tyranny that has ruled over humanity not only for centuries but for thousands of years—the despotism of money!"

At this point, our fallen hero briefly put the glass to his mouth and moistened his lips. The dinner guests looked at each other in alarm and trembled as if they had just been winked at in *Murder in the Dark*. But before an acoustic break could follow, he continued with increased passion:

"To transform Europe from the world's most expensive tomb into a 'cradle of civilization,' as it was called in the transition from antiquity to modern times, the Cradle of the World has to be built. I've decided that, and now it's final! It will be a kind of living monument to human endurance, which has been spun between the two poles of certainty—birth and death—ever since the world has existed. If we leave death aside and visually address the need for a celebration of birth for us and future generations, making use of the total architectural memory of humanity (from the Aztecs to the Far Eastern, Persian, Roman, and European heritage), such a structure is indispensable in our time, for the transition from the second to the third millennium. Yes, dear colleagues, ladies and gentlemen, humanity must create for itself a timeless structure that transcends differences in nation, religion, outlook, color, and background, so that the mistakes of the past are not repeated. We cannot continue the reckless logic of self-destruction, and then apologize that an idea devolved into methodical machinery that killed millions of innocent men, women, and children. Communism set out and devastated half the planet, and seven decades later it's clear that it was a mistake. Fascism set out and perpetrated the blackest crimes ever in history, and it's clear that it was a mistake. Tomorrow turbo-capitalism, the tyranny of money, will set out and also bring about the mass death of individuals, communities, and entire peoples, and afterwards we'll all know it was a mistake . . . We must not allow this at all, for our own sake or for the sake of future generations, and especially for that of all past generations, because one day the innocent victims of all times will arise and the biggest war in human history will be fought—a battle between the dead and the living. And do you know who is sure of victory? Do you know by how many the dead outnumber the living? Can you imagine such a picture? I can, because I survived a fall from a great height! I'm alive thanks to you—the World Construction rescue team's swiftness—and thanks to the impeccable intervention of Professor Rudolf Benn at the neurosurgical department of the Augusta Victoria Hospital, and of course thanks to my dear wife Tsveta who took all the churches of Macedonia in her angelic hands, shaped them into a glowing candle, and prayed for my recovery. And why? So that I can do my duty to Germany and Europe, to world architecture and history, to the world's errors and dreams, to all our ancestors, mothers, fathers, and siblings, close and distant relatives, cousins, uncles and aunts, lovers, colleagues, friends and enemies, acquaintances, and strangers. I'll build the Eighth Wonder of the World with your help, with the help of all those I named, and of course with God's help, because when my father appeared to me in the dream, I realized that God is really nothing but an eternal Father of an eternal student, who is astonished by an incurable disease or marvels at the mystery of existence.

"May God forgive me, but I saw His eyes in the eyes of my father. One thing should be clear: without a father, and especially without a mother, God has no chance of existing. God is in everything, but only once you come into the world. If you don't come into the world, you can't know He exists!

"Now I'll return to the Wonder of the World. Let me share with you some aspects of this structure whose roots go back to the great tradition of Macedonian alchemy in the history of world architecture. We should remember that, way back in the time of Alexander the Great, over 2,300 years ago, Macedonian masons enriched the world of architecture with the principle of 'the impossible as possible.' On April 7, 331 BC, after his visit to the Oracle of Amun in the Siwa Oasis immediately after arriving in Egypt, Alexander had a conversation with his architect, Dinocrates, at the place where he would establish the city of Alexandria.

"'Will it be possible to decorate the Library of Alexandria, which will gather all the world's knowledge, with frescoes or to stretch the facade like a cloth to create a three-dimensional illusion of space in the frontage?'

"'That's impossible!' Dinocrates said.

"'If the impossible is not possible in what we build, I do not want to build a single Alexandria!' the young emperor replied to his architect.

"As we know, seventy-seven Alexandrias were founded in the world in the course of his life—and he lived only to the age of thirty-three, and these cities still bear his name today because Macedonian master craftsmen brought the mystery of the impossible as possible from Egypt via Asia Minor to Bactria, to today's Afghanistan, and on to Persia and India, until it made its way into world architecture!

"But back to the Cradle of the World and its most important elements that you, dear colleagues and witnesses of my fall, will be the first to learn of on the occasion of this, my farewell dinner.

"The Eighth Wonder of the World will rise above a forest of marble columns, 365 in number and 175 feet high, or 53.5 meters, corresponding to the height of the Memorial Church in Berlin, from which I fell and was lucky to survive. Since the number of days in a year is the only number that the whole world agrees on, this will be the common basis that reflects all aspects of historical, social, economic, geographic, and political justice. All days belong equally to all: to all recognized, known, and unknown states, languages, and peoples. Monday is Monday everywhere. Tuesday is Tuesday everywhere. Not to mention Wednesday, Thursday, Friday, Saturday, and Sunday. And that's it; then it's Monday again. The Cradle of the World formed by the columns will be visible from an altitude of 20–30,000 feet, from every plane that flies over Europe. Special flights might even be organized to see it, for example from Berlin to Alexandria, without you having to land in Macedonia if you don't have time. The cradle will rock constantly, making it the only known structure in the history of humanity that is forever in motion, because the marble columns, over which the wooden cradle will rest on steel wires in the empty central space, will be arranged in relation to the prevailing air currents, and these will cause a constant swinging of the human race during its earthly stay.

"More important, all present and future states, members of the United Nations, as well as unrecognized, semi- or para-states, even threatened peoples—except those that have already disappeared—will be able to come and have the names of two kinds of children carved into the great columns in all the 6,703 known languages of the world with the help of specialized stonemasons: the Savior Children, so that they multiply, and the Murderer Children, so that they never come again.

"By way of illustration: let us imagine that a delegation of German humanists, the president of the German parliament or of a region such as North Rhine-Westphalia, visits the Cradle of the World and presents the following proposal: Goethe, Heine, Büchner, and Beethoven are to be engraved on the marble columns of the Savior Children; and Hitler, Goebbels, and Göring on those of the Murderer Children, who have caused great human catastrophes. The specialized masons will carve the names in the white of the stone. Everything will be done in white for the simple reason that world history is not black-and-white. In the beginning, everything is white. Take the birth of a child who, thirty years later, becomes a murderer of millions: does the mother know that her newborn, wrapped in white diapers and surrounded by the joy of family and friends, will later become a monster, killing millions and shrouding a whole epoch in black? Of course not, how could she know? As such, everything is completely white at first, and later it becomes completely black."

Our hero forged through the labyrinth of his thoughts so adroitly that those present followed him most attentively, but also in fear that he might collapse over the dinner table at any moment. But he went on, driven by the urge to express the idea of the Eighth Wonder of the World as clearly as possible—the idea that had taken possession of his jumbled gray cells.

"Dear colleagues, ladies and gentlemen," Alexander continued, "Let me draw your attention to the Holy Water Portal that will be built at the entrance to the Cradle of the World. Each visitor must go into the water, naked or clothed, to be physically purified of their sins of the past and future, as well as their sinful thoughts, in order to reach the Cradle of the World, where the unborn children of the human race will sleep. Here, I must admit, I was influenced by the sacred lake of the temple complex in Karnak, and also the specific Macedonian element in it, especially since Alexander's half-brother, Philip Arrhidaeus, introduced the Macedonian spirit to the architectural alchemy of the Amun-Re cult in 330 BC. After washing, the visitor enters the forest of white marble columns, and now you see what the Eighth Wonder of the World has to offer: a lullaby in one of the 6,703 known languages, from the rich trove of the peoples on planet earth! All the most heavenly lullabies of human history will be played from the acoustic memory of the marble columns. The visitor will be able to hear a song in the language of their choice, and the Cradle of the World itself will pray under the stars. That is the moment when humanity will recognize—not only individually but also collectively—what it most urgently needs right now: a departure from hatred and an embarkment into a new age, where love, tolerance, and mutual understanding between peoples and individuals will rule on earth. After the single visit of any person, word of the existence of the Eighth Wonder of the World will spread from mouth to mouth, from mouth to ear, from one man, woman, child to another, so that every—or almost every—inhabitant of our earth will wonder if they can lead a fulfilled life without having personally seen the only building that celebrates every child born into the world and doesn't differentiate according to skin color, religion, nation, social group, or political affiliation. The message of the Cradle of the World will penetrate the soul of each individual and bring about the biggest upheaval in the history of the human race. Be prepared for a big surprise!"

Here Alexander made a dramatic pause so full of suspense that Tsveta almost had a heart attack.

"Be prepared," he repeated, and everyone in the restaurant became all ears and all eyes. He had the definite impression that not only all of Berlin was listening to him, but also the whole of Europe from the Atlantic to the Urals, as well as the whole of America, Asia, Latin America, and Africa.

But what happened then? A mysterious white figure in a white suit, with white hair and dark glasses—like some latter-day Dracula—with a yellow rosary in his pale hands, stood up from the table in the right-hand corner of the restaurant where he had been sitting alone, went up to World Construction's table, and asked one of Simsar's workmates:

"Who is that?"

"That's our facade artist, who had a serious accident," the man whispered into his white ear. "He fell from the Memorial Church and remained alive!"

The white figure thanked him and went back to his chair.

Fallen Alexander did not notice this event at all and continued enthusiastically:

"When I erect the Eighth Wonder of the World, all the wars in the world will instantly end. The world will enter a long-awaited historic transformation, leading to universal prosperity. All social, spiritual, industrial, and technological differences will cease to be an obstacle to human progress, and the earth, which 'hangs from nothing,' as some of civilization's oldest written sources put it, will be obsessed with delight at discovering the Cradle of the World. All political entities, formations, and structures everywhere will join this edifice and idea, not for the sake of power, which for the first time in history they'll leave lying in the street like an old rag; they'll celebrate birth through lullabies, which will replace all the national anthems, those symbols of conquest; but lullabies are a symbol of the future dream into which humanity will sink. Yes, for the first time in all known epochs of human existence, first hundreds, then thousands, and then millions of people will identify themselves with the word *cradle*, not for reasons of disposition, social origin, color, or religion, not even as a means of striving for power, but solely because of the significance of birth, and the word *cradle* will become the center, the *conditio sine qua non*, the *raison d'être*—the beginning of a new chapter in world history.

"Through the Eighth Wonder of the World, the word *cradle* will open up a new view of human life as a value in itself, whose designation will be derived from the suffix *-ism*, the most common word-formation element in the world: humanism, cosmopolitanism, fascism, capitalism, communism, feudalism, Catholicism, Protestantism, Islamism, Judaism, Buddhism, Machiavellism, Stalinism, Titoism, realism, surrealism, symbolism, neorealism, futurism, anarchism, environmentalism, expressionism, impressionism, and so on. But never has the suffix *-ism* experienced such ecstasy, such an explosion in a truly intimate and at the same time collective act, as you'll see with all those who believe in the humanist message of the Eighth Wonder of the World, its legitimacy, and the need for its construction.

"I'll give a few examples so you can convince yourselves. First, I'll take my home country, Macedonia. The word for *cradle* in Macedonian is *kroshna*, so we call the world view 'kroshnism.'

> In German, *cradle* is *Wiege*—Wiegism
> In Spanish: *cuna*—cunism
> In Italian: *culla*—cullism
> In Russian: *kolybel*—kolybelism
> In Arabic: *mahd*—mahdism
> In Hindi: *jhula*—jhulism
> In Chinese: *noi*—noism
> In English: *cradle*—cradlism
> In French: *berceau*—bercism
> In Japanese: *yurikago*—yurikagism
> In Persian: *nanu*—nanuism
> In Swedish: *vagga*—vaggism
> In Hebrew: *arisa*—arism
> In Turkish: *beşik*—beşkism
> In Armenian: *ororots*—ororotism
> In Tshiluba, a language from Congo: *bulalu bwa mwana*—bulalu bwa mwanism

"The word *cradle* will thus form 6,703 derivatives in all the known and unknown languages of the world. This primal reference of the Eighth Wonder of the World, as well as its structure and particular way of functioning, will ensure that no individual is excluded; moreover, no ethnic, national, or multinational community will be marginalized, not even the smallest tribal group. There will be room for everyone in the Eighth Wonder of the World, which will become a jukebox of the lullaby chords of the entire world community—the source of an unprecedented, unparalleled new humanism.

"A papyrus from 1150 BC mentions that 81,322 workers participated in the construction of the temple complex in Karnak. That is three times less than the number of unemployed in Macedonia today. If I then add the unemployed in a number of Balkan countries or throughout Eastern Europe, together with the construction teams that will have nothing to build after the collapse of communism, the disbanding of superfluous armies, and the abolition of the arms industry, I don't see why I shouldn't invite them to work on a voluntary basis in one of the oldest marble quarries, near the Macedonian city of Prilep. I have irrefutable evidence that this marble was used by Phidias and Alexander the Great's architect, but also by the builders of all the empires that passed through Macedonia. Why shouldn't I also invite the unemployed from the normal, capitalist countries, volunteers who believe in the humane principles of a new age, in which we'll rediscover ourselves— all of us, who until yesterday were divided between rich north and poor south?

"When the Cradle of the World is ready, I'll invite all of you gathered at this table. And not only you: I'll invite all the living and dead on earth, because the Eighth Wonder of the World will be built only once, just as I fell from Berlin's Memorial Church only once, and remained alive!"

And he emptied his glass to the last drop.

Everyone present at the dinner in Goethe's Garden stood up at that moment and toasted their remarkable friend. His beloved wife, Tsveta, stood by his side, overflowing with indescribable happiness, and although she did not understand what he had said in German, she put her hand on his shoulder, looked up at him, and wept.

Deeply moved by the words of the facade artist, Hans Neubauer embraced the Simsars with both arms. Then he spoke:

"Dear colleagues, ladies and gentlemen, just as Germany must never forget the fall of the Berlin Wall or your fall, my dear Alexander 'the Great,' Europe as a whole must never forget that decline and fall have been a fundamental component of its history. Nothing must be allowed to pass into oblivion. Nor may the tears of your beautiful wife be forgotten, for you fell and survived, and I see no reason why the structure you dream of and call the Eighth Wonder of the World should not come to fruition. All of us here tonight, the whole of World Construction, in which you have selflessly invested your whole working life, and—if I may be so bold—all of Germany, yes, the whole world, must stand behind you! May God in heaven look down on you and grant you health, happiness, and love, and may the first child to rock in the Cradle of the World be your child!"

Alexander's official farewell to Germany took its course. All the administrative, medical, proprietary, and financial matters were resolved. A pension transfer letter was issued, he clarified all the remaining questions at the hospital, gave notice on the apartment in Kreuzberg, and withdrew the twenty years' savings from his Deutsche Bank account: 596,292 marks.

In his mind, he turned all the money to marble. That stone began to beat in his heart at 8 a.m. on January 7, 1990, the Orthodox Christmas Day, when he and Tsveta arrived at Berlin airport for their flight via Vienna to Skopje. After they had passed through customs and were walking over the tarmac to the waiting Boeing 707, he looked up at the ramp as the first passengers were entering the plane. Those mobile stairs, reminiscent of scaffolding, suddenly reminded him strongly of the construction site at the Memorial Church, which he had not visited again since the accident. In his heart, the stone of his savings beat for the Eighth Wonder of the World, the Cradle of the World, in which he wished to invest his whole future life. This déjà vu stirred and unsettled him, since scaffolding was a key element of his professional, spiritual, and to some extent medical destiny. Actually, all he had to do was climb the ramp and board the plane to take his comfortable seat. But then, in his head, the ramp turned into a launch pad for direct passage into the sky. It seemed to him that all of Europe was tied in a kind of Gordian knot with the two Americas, Asia and Africa, the small continents and archipelagoes; this vision in the very left corner of his brain completely blocked our hero's motion center. Tsveta was on the ramp already, but he remained on the tarmac. A black leather bag he had bought in Amsterdam's *Doodstraat*—Death Street—exactly ten years earlier now hung from his right shoulder and contained all the designs for the construction projects he had devised but never realized. He reached over his head to check if he was back on a scaffold ladder he needed to climb. Did it exist or didn't it? At that moment, believe it or not, the figure in the white suit appeared before him, with white hair and white eyebrows, white eyes and white teeth, with a white mouth and white tongue, white shirt and white tie, with a yellow rosary in his hands and dark glasses. He spoke to the fallen man:

"Are you Alexander Simsar?"

"Yes."

"Allow me to introduce myself: Satanael Devil Shaitan Teufel Hudich Diabolus Gubernator Mundi—Envoy of the New World Order and the White Trade International!"

"Pleased to meet you."

"Are you absolutely mad?"

"No, I'm fine."

"Are you sure?"

"Oh, yes!"

"And after the fall: are you in your right mind?"

"It's true that I had a fall some time ago, but my mind is all there. I haven't lost my marbles!"

"Well, I can assure you that, according to the specialist report commissioned by the White Trade International, the contents of your brain evaporated completely in the fall. The best evidence is your confused speech at the farewell dinner in Goethe's Garden!"

"Why?"

"What do you mean *why*, you stupid skydiver? How can you not understand the most basic things about the course of world history? After decades of struggle by the entire international community, the utopia of world communism has definitely collapsed, we see the ruins all about us, the dust has scarcely settled, and you dare to announce a new utopia!"

"I haven't announced anything. All I said was that I'm going to build the Eighth Wonder of the World, the Cradle of the World. That's not a utopia—it's the truth!"

"The moment you translated the word *cradle* into English, Arabic, Russian, French, German, Spanish, Chinese, Japanese, and Portuguese, you were in effect calling for a new alliance of the disenfranchised layers of the world's population against private capitalism!"

"You know, Mr. Satanael Devil Shaitan Teufel Hudich Diabolus Gubernator Mundi, White Envoy of the New World Order and the White Trade International, I translated the word because of the lullabies. No revolution in the world was ever incited with a lullaby, and no utopia is based on falling asleep. Utopias are always an awakening—but I call for sleep!"

"Now listen to me, let's keep this short and sweet. Go back to Macedonia and rest. You've worked for years all over the world. Enjoy the beauty of nature, dedicate yourself to your wife, and even have a child if you can. You prattled on about the Cradle of the World, the Eighth Wonder of the World, and similar nonsense in Berlin; you won't repeat that performance, either in this world or the next. If you do, I'll come zooming up in your scrambled head and hoist you up the launch pad that's just appeared in your empty, vaporized brain; I'll crush you, feed you through a meat grinder, and throw you down a second time so you're finished once and for all! You're out of the race, but unfortunately you still exist. A very good bye!"

With those words the White Envoy of the New World Order and the White Trade International, Satan Devil Shaitan Teufel Hudich Diabolus Gubernator Mundi, disappeared from before his eyes.

Tsveta ran down the ramp to fetch him and held his hand as he spoke. She didn't understand his words because he spoke German, but she knew he was alone, and yet he stood there petrified. A river of German flowed from his mouth, in which she recognized only the fatal word *cradle*.

"Come on, my angel," she said. "The ramp will be pushed backed any minute!"

"Sorry," he muttered, "I thought someone came up to me, stopped in front of the ramp, and talked to me!"

"There was nobody, nobody at all," she assured him.

A flight attendant called to them one last time to come aboard so she could close off the ramp. And when Alexander put his right foot on the first step, he really did not know whether he had died on the sidewalk in front of the Memorial Church in Berlin, or whether he was returning to Macedonia as a living master builder who had conquered death.

2.0 Seconds

You should have seen our fallen hero Alexander Simsar sitting 30,000 feet up in German airspace with his seat belt fastened. An expression of immortality had settled on his face and a thought he could not place began to circle unexpectedly in his concussed head: *An idea that is not dangerous, cannot be called an idea at all!* Where had he read about it? Yes, the idea of the Eighth Wonder of the World had turned out to be dangerous, especially in connection with the word *cradle*, and even more so with the sudden appearance of the Envoy of the New World Order and the White Trade International just before he boarded the plane, who accused him of nothing less than launching a new world utopia!

Was he entitled to believe in himself?

Yes.

Could that be an expression of human progress?

No.

Could flying prevent him from believing that he could walk across the sky?

No.

Was his wife, whom he loved above all else, by his side?

Yes.

Would the building faithfully reproduce the image from his dream before the fall?

Yes.

Did God intervene to save him?

Without any doubt!

Those were the thoughts of fallen Alexander Simsar as they flew over Leipzig. He took his wife's hand with great tenderness and said: "Hold your ear to my head. Johann Sebastian Bach is playing inside because his grave lies here below us. My message has reached him and now, to encourage me in my project, he's playing his Mass in B minor and telling me: *Build the Eighth Wonder of the World and fear no one!* Can you hear him?"

"Yes, I can hear him playing in your head, quite loudly. Turn it down, if you like."

"Dear Mr. Bach, I thank you for participating and supporting the new architectural jewel of world history that will grow in Macedonia!"

The plane flew on and Alexander hovered in a kind of trance that the classical music had evoked in his memory.

"Rest, my love," he told his wife. "When we approach Prague, I'll strike up Smetana's *My Homeland* at the very moment the plane flies over the Charles Bridge."

Here she unexpectedly burst into laughter and began kissing her fallen husband everywhere: on his hair, his eyes, his face, his suit, even on his seat belt. And as she petted him, he went to sleep as gently as a lamb.

But nothing in his dream was like the music of Bach, whom they had flown over, or Smetana, whose home city they were gradually approaching, or Mozart, whose bones were finishing a requiem in the common grave in Vienna, still some way off. Nothing was remotely like music. He was being dragged down the long corridor of an administrative building named "Franz K." by a soldier in an unfamiliar uniform. He was flung into a dark cell, and there he remained, knee-deep in water between piles of corpses, naked and alone.

Who are these bodies? This must be a misunderstanding, and a tragic one! he thought, and shouted to the guard: "Hey, out there! I'm not dead. I may have had a bad fall in Berlin, but I didn't die. I'm still alive!"

Suddenly the heavy iron lock of the cell opened. A bronze Buddha statue from 480 BC entered, lit a lantern, and spoke to him in Hindi:

"You called me?"

Our fallen hero almost shat himself in fear.

"N-n-no, Lord Buddha, I didn't call you."

"You are in sorrow," the Buddha said to him.

"Yes, I am. That's very true," Alexander answered.

He wondered: *how is it that I know this language? Until yesterday, I couldn't say a word, and now I can.* He just couldn't think of the word for *cradle* in the Buddha's language. He wanted to tell him about his plan to build the Eighth Wonder of the World—the Cradle of the World—but try as he would, he couldn't come up with the word. The Buddha raised his bronze hand:

"I know you want to build! In order to start, one condition is crucial!"

"What is that?" the fallen man asked.

"Have you harmed any creature?"

"No, neither people nor birds, beasts nor plants, not one!"

"Build, then," the Buddha said. "But as a meditation on

infinity, you must include four elements in the construction of the Eighth Wonder of the World. First of all, Love."

"Yes, Lord Buddha," Alexander answered immediately. "I'm in love with my wife! Love isn't a problem at all, neither at a private nor a collective level. My heart beats for the whole world. Love won't be a problem at all."

"Secondly, Empathy with the suffering of others."

"I suffer!" fallen Alexander said. "Wherever people are killed, I die too. I suffer for all people in this world!"

"Thirdly, Partaking in Joy."

"Yes, joy! The Eighth Wonder of the World will be a monument to joy. No one is more pleased than I about every new child that comes into the world, because I still don't have a child of my own. On the other hand, I don't know if you've been told, Lord Buddha: I survived a fall from a great height. My very existence is cause for joy."

"Fourthly, Inner Purification that frees from suffering and opens the way to truth."

"Yes," Alexander said, "I'm pure inside because I've been working on tall buildings for years, eating only a few vegetables, fish, and two or three types of fruit. I'm purified, freed from suffering, and have seen the way of truth."

The bronze Buddha studied him from tip to toe.

"Can you renounce yourself?"

"Self-renunciation is very familiar to me!" Alexander replied.

"Build then!" the Buddha said and reached out his bronze hand.

"Please give it to me in black and white, Lord Buddha! You've now given me your permission, but I have to prove that what I intend to build is, in your eyes, not a little trifle but a project of global relevance, and if the peoples of Asia ask me how the Buddha approved it, I'll be able to produce the document and say: 'Look, sahib, I have it in black and white.'"

Then the Buddha stroked our hero on the head with his right hand and spoke:

"Open your left hand!"

Alexander opened his left hand. Black ink flowed from the Buddha's bronze forefinger and wrote on the palm of his hand: *Shakyamuni*—Sage of the Tribe of Shakya, and at that very moment he disappeared. Alexander remained alone in his dream again. The uniformed guard pushed the door open again and introduced another visitor: he was clad in a long robe and carried a heavy book in his hands.

"Warden, I don't know where I am, not even in which country. And who is this?" fallen Alexander asked politely.

"This is Moses—from the thirteenth century BC. He wants to see you for a moment!"

"You know, Lord Moses, I'm a simple man from the Balkans. I went out into the wide world to . . ."

Moses raised his hand and spoke:

"My fallen child! I have seen you from far away, from very far away. I noticed you long ago, maybe even as far back as your father's funeral and the dream you had back then. I have watched you for years and know everything about you. You do not need to tell me anything. I follow the fate of Macedonia closely. I and my Jewish people will never forget Macedonia for everything it has done for us! For over 2,600 years, Jews have been living in your homeland, ever since the campaign of Darius I in 513 BC. Then, in 140 BC, many Jews fled from Alexandria to Macedonia, after having taken sides in the civil war between the Macedonian[1] queen Cleopatra and her enemies. And let us not forget that the first tombstone bearing the name of Abraham was discovered around that time in the vicinity of Thessaloniki, formerly known as Salonika. In the early Roman Empire, the first synagogue was established on European soil in Macedonia, and in 1492 Macedonia took in 500,000 Jews expelled by Isabella, who from then on spoke Ladino in Salonika, Kastoria, Ohrid, Shtip, Bitola, and Skopje, and as a result Jewish culture blossomed again for five centuries in the Balkans."

"I can even sing you a song in Ladino!" And at this point in his dream, fallen Alexander began to sing a song for Moses:

En este mundo sin valor
Como me topo no intiendo
Arvoles lloran por lluvia
y montaños por aiere
Ay momentos que nose loque me pasa
Tengo ganos de reir i de llorar
Adio, adio querida
no quero la vida

---

1 Cleopatra's dynasty was founded by Ptolemy, a general under Alexander the Great

(Why, why am I here
In this worthless world?
The woods are crying for the rain
and the mountains for the wind.
Sometimes I do not know what I feel
I want to laugh and cry.
Farewell, farewell, my love,
I am tired of life.)

Moses looked at him and cried.

"What do you want to build?" he asked Alexander.

"The Eighth Wonder of the World! But I'm worried: there is a white figure with eyebrows, hair, eyes—all white—who is stalking me!"

"No one can harm you," Moses said to him, opening the heavy, leather-bound book. "See to your path and your building. Whenever your heart is heavy, remember my tears."

"Lord Moses, forgive me, but could you possibly leave some sign as proof that you have seen me and approved of my edifice, so that no one dares endanger it?"

Moses wet his right finger on his wet eye and ordered:

"Open your left hand."

Fallen Alexander opened it and Moses made a sign with his index finger, and then he disappeared from the dream, as if the earth had swallowed him up.

"I have to tell you, Lord Moses, that I read Freud's work *Moses and Monotheism* and disagreed with some of the statements, for example . . . Hello, are you still here?"

The key turned in the heavy lock and the cell door in the Franz K. administrative building opened again. The guard in the unfamiliar uniform told the prisoner: "There is a man here who says he has come from far away to see you. He didn't mention his name. Will you receive him?"

Before Alexander could speak in his dream, he saw an untold brightness illuminate the dark corridors he had been brought through. He saw millions of men, women, and children locked up in cells like he was, and they were all waiting for Him to come, but He did not. Alexander waited too. But lo and behold, now He came to see him! Alexander recognized Him, he was sure about it, but he dared not pronounce His name; it was Jesus Christ, who had come to prison as a special envoy of God, who is one. In his dream, fallen Alexander believed that this honor was being shown to him alone of all living creatures, plants, and beasts of the earth, and he wanted to shout and let the whole world know: *Look here, everyone: I fell from the Memorial Church in Berlin and survived, and not only that, but I now have the chance to try and win Jesus Christ personally for the construction of the Eighth Wonder of the World! For, as we know, He has taken all the sins of humanity in the last 2,000 years upon himself to save each and every one of us, not only in the past—because in the past we are all basically saved—but also in the future. That's the issue now!*

He also wanted to say: *I swear to you on the grave of my father and mother, and I swear on my wife and only love who is by my side right now, that I saw Jesus Christ, in the flesh, from head to foot, with the same eyes and face, a mirror of the world, with a long colorful robe inscribed with various alphabets—the holy scripts of lost and almost completely forgotten peoples.*

The robe looked to have been woven of Babylonian cloth, its colors mingled, and the fallen man began to count them: one, two, three . . . sixteen . . . twenty-seven. He knew that Herakleia Lynkestis, one of the cities founded by Philip II of Macedonia when Alexander was only seven years old, had an early Christian mosaic with twenty-seven different colors of stones, and he wanted to say to Jesus Christ: *On your robe, o son of man, is sown the hope for all living creatures, for humans, plants, and beasts. Give them all hope—and also to me, your fallen son!*

But he said none of all this; he opened his mouth, and just imagine what came out:

"O Jesus Christ, our God, I swear I will tell no one and that it will stay between us: will you allow me to build the Eighth Wonder of the World?"

Christ did not answer, of course. He produced a sack of straw from beneath the Babylonian garment of twenty-seven colors and scattered it in the cell in the dream of humble, fallen Alexander. It turned out that He had also come with a wooden suitcase, from which He took out a small wooden table and placed it in front of Alexander; then he took out a wooden bowl of cheese with a lid, put it on the table, and got out a bottle of wine. While Alexander wondered how a bottle could survive the long journey from Jerusalem unscathed, Jesus produced two glasses and finally two stools; He handed one to his host, sat down on the other, and said:

"Please sit down, you tormented, fallen, and personally rescued soul."

"O Jesus Christ, our God, how do I deserve the honor of sitting with you like this in confidence?"

Jesus Christ poured wine into the two glasses, raised His and said:

"One of those who is here now will see the coming of the Son of Man before he dies. His kingdom will come—it is already here!"

Alexander, with glass raised as well, asked the Savior:

"Bless my building, dear God—the Cradle of the World or the Eighth Wonder of the World that I want to build in Macedonia. You have personally saved me and I ask you to endorse my venture in black and white!"

"Everyone should know, you included, that at the end of the world the sun will be darkened, the moon will not give its light, and the stars will fall from the sky."

"That's right," Alexander said. "Of course they should know that."

"And only he should rejoice, for whom my second coming will be no reason for the ultimate fall!"

"But Lord Jesus, Son of Man and Son of God, please bear in mind that I have already fallen. And not only that, but when I fell I had that dream. I dreamt of the whole of humanity and then I set out to turn that dream into stone. But there is one thing I wish to tell you, and you alone: I won't begin building the Eighth Wonder of the World without your blessing. You know, there is a terrible misunderstanding. Ever since the banquet in Berlin, a strange creature with white hair, white forehead, white eyes, white eyebrows, white teeth, white suit, white ears—but dark glasses—has been following me and appears to me in certain, totally unexpected moments and says: 'I'll crush you and feed you through a mincer, you threaten the world with your new utopia!' Lord Jesus, I can't explain the dreadful force with which it reached out its white right hand with its white index finger and told me: 'The past is the past. History has seen enough utopias. From now on, trade will determine the future. Everything has already been said, repeated, and re-repeated; the history of civilization is just an echo chamber. And because that is so, no one can question the New World Order any more, least of all with a utopia, a creation, or, if you like, an idea! Who needs such nonsense? You've seen what such ideas lead to! 'The cradle, the cradle, the cradle,' you'll wax poetic, and in no time you'll set upon the world; instead of the communists, you cradlists, or whatever you call yourselves, will drive the world to rack and ruin!' That's what the strange pale figure told me, Lord Jesus. What's more, he said: 'If you build the Eighth Wonder of the World I'll crush you—no, I'll beat you up and chop you into little pieces.' I wanted to answer: *Please remember that I've had a bad fall. My building doesn't question world trade and the tyranny of money at all . . .* If you, Lord Jesus, your mother Mary and your father, our God, could all help me now to save myself from that white menace, I'd be eternally grateful; not only me, but also my wife. I'm very surprised that everything about that figure is white . . ."

Jesus Christ raised his hands from his Babylonian robe of twenty-seven colors, and at once twenty-seven suns began to radiate in different colors and cast their glistening light into

Alexander's eyes. He wondered how Jesus could suddenly make so many colors—*he's not an impressionist painter!* Then Jesus reached his right hand deep into his breast and said:

"Now I will tell you why the Envoy of the New World Order is white, dear Alexander Simsar. He is white because my heart has been turning black and blacker for nearly 2,000 years—as black as black can be! Two thousand years after I was born, after I drove the merchants out of the temple in Jerusalem, they've turned the planet into one big marketplace; they buy and sell countries, nations, and religions; the depravity of capitalism is crescendoing into an international orgy, millions of human beings are dying of hunger, and I have to watch it day and night, for years, for millennia, my fallen Alexander!"

Jesus gradually drew his hand out from under his Babylonian robe, which shone in twenty-seven colors. And imagine, dear reader, what he took out and laid on the little wooden table: his black heart.

Alexander almost died of agitation in his dream; but he didn't die.

Jesus continued: "If the devil's representative appears in your poor head, just think of my black heart. All the forms of the white terrorism of Capitalism, which since the fall of Communism have set about buying up two-thirds of the globe for a pittance and are embodied in an agent by the name of Satanael Devil Shaitan Teufel Hudich Diabolus Gubernator Mundi, will instantly disappear from your thoughts! All I have been able to do in these 2,000 years is to drive evil out of people's thoughts, but I can do nothing about the evil itself.

Therefore, touch my black, burned, charred heart with your finger and return to Macedonia: build the Eighth Wonder of the World or the Cradle of the World. I agree!"

"But can't you give it to me in black and white?" fallen Alexander asked with his all-too-mortal stubbornness.

"I let you touch my black heart; that is my will. Take my black heart with you into the white infinity of that human-made hell of commerce, where love will soon be snuffed out. May the Eighth Wonder of the World, which you have conceived, renew the shattered foundations of love. That is my blessing for you, Alexander Simsar."

No sooner had he spoken those words than he disappeared.

"Lord Jesus, I cannot express what satisfaction this encounter brings me. But why are you abandoning me so abruptly? It reminds me of how you yourself called out *Eli, Eli, lama sabachtani*, My God, my God, why have you forsaken me? I'm not saying you don't know what it means to fall—we know that you fell three times under the weight of the cross on the way to Golgotha—but my fall is not to be underestimated; there was no cross, but I fell from a steeple, a full 53.5 meters high. It was the Memorial Church . . ."

But there was no one left in his dream, where now he saw a black dot on the tip of his right index finger as if he had held his finger in a blazing fire, and he almost wanted to put his finger in his mouth to relieve the stinging pain. He looked down the dark corridors and saw that two guards were leading a fourth visitor. Soon they unlocked the door again and brought him to our fallen hero in his wet charnel house of a cell.

When one of the guards shut the door again, Alexander asked him if there would be another visit afterwards.

"No, this is the last one for now."

And who do you think it was, dear reader? In a caftan and with a turban on his head, with a beard that he had seen in the Mevlana mosque in Konya, Turkey, He now stood before Alexander in the cell: the champion and founder of Islam!

"*Bismillahi rahmani rahim* . . . Oh, Mohammed, I'll never forget this moment. But how is it that you appear to me?"

Mohammed spoke Arabic. Fallen Alexander could speak no Arabic, yet he understood every word. *The fall from the Memorial Church seems to have brought me nothing but advantages*, he thought. *The main thing is that I'm still alive, and I'm as good as unharmed. Secondly, I can now understand all the languages in the world. It seems God in heaven is preparing me personally for the construction of the Eighth Wonder of the World and, in a word, sent me these four unexpected visitors one after another.*

Now Mohammed said to him: "I have chosen to visit you because you love all people in this world without distinction of faith, color, or nation. When my earthly ministries informed me of your speech in Berlin, with the announcement that for the first time in human history there would be such a temple, where a 'Cradle of the World' would rock, I said to myself: *That's not a bad idea at all, and I shall find ways and means to support the construction project!* I found out the address of the 'Franz K.' building, albeit with difficulty, and so here I am, visiting you in this prison, from which you will soon be released. I wish to encourage you on your path. You strike me as very similar to the Sufis in Islam. As if your father were the great fourteenth-century Anatolian poet Yunus Emre or, no—before him, the Persian thinker Omar Khayyam who said: 'How long will it be narrow, so unbearably narrow, in myself?', and 'Who is he, who finds the gate of his own abyss by himself?' And also: 'He who finds the gate in himself will transform it into eternity!' That is characteristic of you as well. You resemble Abraham, the father of the Jews, Christians, and Muslims. He can say to them all today: I will make children of stone—not of you, because you are flesh and blood, and nothing else. You have no children, so you dream of stone!"

Here Mohammed fell silent. *All the prophets know I have no children*, thought Alexander, horrified, and buried his fingers in his hair; the two guards stood there petrified, one on the left and one on the right. Mohammed spoke again:

"You'll now go by what we in Islam call *al-salaf al-salih*: purity through the tears of the ancients. You do not have to be a Muslim for that; you have to find a path back to the good way, *al-huda*, and return, so to speak, to the beginning—the 'time of initiation.' All this corresponds to the description of the Cradle of the World that you gave in Berlin. I do not think it contradicts the philosophy of Islam in any way. You can build the Eighth Wonder of the World unhindered. It shall be approved of by the many millions of Muslims in the world!"

Fallen Alexander looked the prophet in the eye. The guards seemed impatient. Mohammed straightened his turban, arranged his caftan, and asked:

"Is there anything else before we part?"

Brimming with enthusiasm, Alexander wanted to tell the prophet—or did he actually say it?—nobody can know:

"I must apologize that you had to undertake such a long journey for my sake."

Mohammed looked at him almost reproachfully: "No, really. This is an indescribable pleasure for me. It really puts me in a festive mood when I see people on the run, like you. I once was too: I fled from Mecca to Medina; therefore I know what flight or escape is—*hegira*. I need no one to tell me what jihad is! *Al-jihad al-akbar*, I am on the holy path in the fight against myself! I know that, too, so you should feel no regret. Just as you have built and restored churches, mosques, holy and secular temples of every kind all over the world, so I have watched the traders happily passing by throughout Arabia, from Yemen to Syria, and I have listened to what they all talked about, what the Chinese, Byzantines, Persians, and Jews spoke about among themselves in the endless caravans of the Silk Road. I have studied the world written in heaven, and the Angel with the holy finger showed me the way to God! And Khadijah, my first wife, with whom I had seven children, said to me: 'Fear not, believe you are the one and no one else! You can count on my aid at any time! Wherever I am, if you think of me I'll hear your cry for help!'"

"You know, Lord Mohammed, before you leave, I must urgently ask you to help. Just when I wanted to board the plane in Berlin, a completely white figure appeared in front of me on the tarmac at the foot of the ramp. He threatened me not to think of the building I've dreamed of, otherwise I'd be chopped into little pieces, ground to mince, and thrown on the dunghill! I can show you if you like: the guy gave me a business card with his branches all over the world. He's an envoy of the White Trade International and the New World Order and, like I said, he's so white that it's hard to see him; and he warns that it's dangerous for the world to believe in a new utopia. And now see what's happened: he wants to make me, of all people, into mincemeat. Me, after my bad fall! Does he know no sin? I can't really describe him, or only roughly. Everything about him is white: his eyes, brows, nose, mouth, teeth, hair—everything is white, through and through . . . What I'd like to know is: Can you free me from this white curse?"

Mohammed straightened his turban and tightened his caftan. He did not reply at first. One of the guards sneezed. *That means my wife is thinking of me*, Alexander said to himself, and addressed his request to Mohammed once more:

"This white figure could destroy my life's dream, not only for me, but for all of Macedonia, all of Europe, and the whole world!"

Mohammed touched our fallen hero on the forehead and said:

"Whenever the White Envoy of the White Trade International appears to you in spirit, make this movement with both hands: raise them, let them sink back down, and round off the movement as if you were drawing a black square: it looks like the Black Stone *Al-Hajar al-Aswad* in the Kaaba, the Al-Haram Mosque in Mecca. The Black Stone possesses a magical power to break the relentless 'white forces' of history embodied in remorseless commerce. May the Black Stone of the Kaaba protect you on your way to building the Cradle of the World, your future!"

And then Mohammed headed for the door. Alexander wanted to fall to his knees, but that was hardly possible knee-deep in the water between piles of dead bodies.

"You know, Lord Mohammed, when I was in Mecca for the first time with the German firm World Construction, I touched the black stone. Back then, I did not believe it fell from the sky, but now I believe it because I know what a fall is!"

The guards exchanged glances and unlocked the door; Mohammed went out first and they followed straight after. No sooner had the iron key turned in the heavy lock three times and he was alone again in the dungeon cell, naked as a newborn and knee-deep in rotten human remains, then a powerful jet of water suddenly spewed into the cell, knocking him off balance and almost carrying him away. He kept the Buddha's signet and the sign of Moses in his left hand, in his right the trace of the black heart of Jesus Christ and the black square of Mohammed, and when all the doors opened in the dark corridor of the administrative building, he was standing in a speedy chariot, like that of the hero Arjuna from the *Gita*, the sacred book he had read in German seven or eight years ago, the book of over a billion Hindus, in which Arjuna speaks with Vishnu-Krishna about the justification of fratricidal war everywhere in the world. A seemingly endless battlefield stretched before his eyes, and in his dream he began to bemoan his fate after the fall, and to shout loudly:

"Hey, what the hell is going on? Why do I have to sit here like a bum in the dirt?! A Buddhist, Jesusist, Mosesist, Mohammedist, Krishnaist . . . What am I, and why am I in this fucking mess? Aaarg!"

His scream frightened the crew and the other passengers on the Berlin-Vienna-Skopje trip, up in the airspace between Bratislava and Vienna. He awoke in the arms of his beloved Tsveta, who was wiping sweat from his forehead.

"What did you dream, sweetheart?" she asked him.

"I was given permission to build—by all five!"

"Which five?"

"I met Buddha, Moses, Jesus, Mohammed, and Krishna in person, and you could even say that I not only obtained their approval for the construction but also achieved something of a spiritual consensus! This isn't a fantasy, I want you to know—I have it in black and white!"

"What do you mean, black and white?"

He opened the palms of his hands, made a black square with his hands, pointed to the black signature of the Buddha, the black mark of Moses, the black heart of Jesus, the black stone of Mohammed, and the black chariot of Krishna.

Her lips trembled and it was hard to tell if she was about to smile or cry. She took both his hands and began to lick his fingers, one by one, and to suck on them as well, so that fallen Alexander, after his beatitude, now felt a surge of erotic bliss. For a moment he thought that, having survived the fall, he was allowed to do anything, and if Tsveta continued to suck on his fingers, they could start to make love right there in the plane. He even started undressing so as to celebrate the divine approval of the construction in his dream with such an act, but that lasted only a moment, of course, because Tsveta knew him very well, both before and after his fall: he could be quick to get to the point. She almost saw herself with her legs spread at 30,000 feet after he had come up with the idea of taking her right there with a view of Vienna; perhaps in honor of the pauper's grave that Mozart was thrown into, or a building like the Belvedere palace, which turned his head as he worked on its facades. He had stood high up in the scaffolding in so many cities of the world, and she had prayed that God might protect him from death by making one false move in a moment of weakness—a perpetual danger. Suddenly, as if frightened, she raised her head, pressed both his hands together with unexpected strength, and asked:

"Did you really see Jesus Christ?"

"I certainly did!"

"Do you know what day it is today?"

"No."

"According to the Orthodox calendar, today is Christmas, the birthday of Jesus. Let me dry the sweat from your forehead that comes from the dream where you saw him, and I'll say the solemn words to you that have been spoken in Macedonia for centuries; but only when you've wiped your brow."

And she spoke to him in the plane over Vienna:

"Christ is born!"

"Truly, He is born!" fallen Alexander answered.

They held each other's hands and felt that Jesus Christ and the others around Him—the angels, servants, apostles, saints, and all the company of heaven—would surely hear their prayers this time; their child would leave the temple of God and come to them to be born, for they had not sinned against God in any way and there was no reason for them to be deprived of offspring as a punishment.

"How is it possible," Alexander said, "that millions of children are born, but none to us?!"

"You never dreamed of Jesus before. From now on, we're in God's hands!"

"I swear to you that I saw Him, and now I blame myself for not congratulating him on his birthday. He was sitting as close to me as you are now. *Forgive me, Son of God, I didn't even think at the time that it's Christmas according to the Orthodox calendar, but you must be lenient with me: I've had a bad fall, remember, and since then I've been confusing the festivals and holidays. Sometimes I even mix up Christmas and Easter, or Pentecost and Ascension, Resurrection and Assumption, St. Leontia and St. Nicholas Day, St. Peter and Paul's Feast and St. John's Day, but I'll turn every day into columns, and so the Eighth Wonder of the World will have 365, and the cradle will rock on 365 days, for every day is God's day, and every day on earth is a gift to us all. Forgive me, o Lord, but . . . please send us a child; arrange it with your colleagues who also visited me in my dream; if you bless us with a child, we'll give the earth a building in which your eternity will be celebrated, for we are mortal and you—everlasting."*

Tsveta stood in front of her husband there on the plane as if before God Himself. She crossed herself when he began to sing because the song had three voices like a choir, although he alone was singing. Then he unbuckled his seat belt, got up, and informed their fellow passengers that it was Orthodox Christmas, and so he'd sing "Glory to God in the highest, and on earth peace, good will toward men" from Luke 2:14. When his three-part choir resounded in Old Church Slavic, the other passengers thought he was an opera singer traveling to perform in Vienna after having given concerts in Berlin.

One of them, who spoke German with a Russian accent, heard the Slavic lyrics and thought Alexander was the world-famous Russian tenor Vladimir Vasilyevich Galuzin; he hurried toward him, kissed him firmly on the forehead, and said:

"Honored Vladimir Vasilyevich, all of Vienna will melt with awe and wonder at your voice!"

Another passenger came up to him from business class, introduced himself as retired US admiral, and said to him in German:

"Sir, your melancholy Russian voice reminds me of my youthful years during the Cold War. We actually had good military cooperation with Moscow, you mustn't think it was otherwise. I recall the fantastic New Year's Eve performance of Tchaikovsky's opera *The Queen of Spades* at the Bolshoi Theater in 1960. I thought at the time, and I still think today, that if Russia stops singing, humanity will perish!"

"You know, gentlemen, I'm not Russian," Alexander explained in German. "The Old Church Slavic language, in which the first liturgy for the Slavic peoples was held—in Rome in 864 AD, to be exact—came from Salonika, from my

country Macedonia, because the monastic brothers Cyril and
Methodius were from there. It was they who brought literature
and culture to all the peoples of the Slavic world: Russians,
Ukrainians, Belarusians, Czechs, Poles, Slovenes, Bulgarians,
Serbs, Croats, and so on. Without Salonika and without
Macedonia, there would have been no entry into civilization!"

"So you're not the Russian tenor Vladimir Galuzin?" asked
the gentleman who spoke German with a Russian accent.

"No, I'm afraid not."

"I'm sorry."

The American admiral also apologized cordially, but
admitted that he'd be immensely happy if Alexander sang
another aria:

"For me, as I spent my entire professional life during the
Cold War, there were two powers in the world: America and
Russia. America was responsible for the production of wealth,
Russia for the production of suffering, and suffering is the
source of pure spirit. You are a pure spirit, and therefore I
want to hear your wonderful voice."

Alexander kissed Tsveta on the lips and said to the
passengers in German:

"Ladies and gentlemen, I'm not an opera singer and I
won't be performing in Vienna, as many of you flatteringly
thought. My path and my purpose have nothing in common
with the art of opera, although I think most highly of it. Given
my attachment to Mozart and everything to do with him as
a phenomenon, and since we're about to begin our approach
to his city, I'll sing a song for you, which Wolfgang Amadeus

heard from a collector of folk music, who had traveled from Constantinople via Venice to Vienna, shortly before he departed for the grave:

> *My eyes have*
> *seen the Savior,*
> *in the company of the four prophets.*
> *And Jesus spoke,*
> *Truly, I say to you:*
> *I am born and the words*
> *of the prophet Isaiah*
> *still weigh heavy on me:*
> *With whom will you compare me*
> *or count me equal?*
> *To whom will you liken me?"*

After his aria, which ended with this questioning crescendo, thunderous applause filled the plane. Two flight attendants with their blue caps went along the aisles and each passenger donated a few coins for the musical contribution of the nameless architect of the Eighth Wonder of the World. The extraordinary musical talent he demonstrated struck not only the other passengers, but also his own wife. He wanted to say a few more words about the Cradle of the World and even tell his listeners about the fall in Berlin—that he had escaped a thousand-percent certain death—but the crew announced that the plane was approaching Vienna airport for landing and insisted that all passengers be seated, with their belts fastened.

They landed, spent thirty minutes in transit, and were transferred to the connecting flight. Our master builder nodded off and slept almost until the plane's arrival in Macedonian airspace, and there is no way of telling whether he dreamed or not because everything was absolutely unpredictable: his sleep and dreams and wakings, his past and his future. Everything was mixed up and seething in his brain: the persistent image of the fall, the thought of his great edifice, and his words— every utterance at a mental, physical, spiritual, and perhaps erotic level—all this was intimately intertwined with the unpredictability of his actions. For example, after he fell asleep and slept like a log for a short while in the transit zone at Vienna airport, boarded the plane to Skopje half asleep, and then continued to sleep during the flight, how did he know so precisely that the plane had entered Macedonian airspace?

"We've just flown into Macedonian airspace!" he said to Tsveta at that very moment. "Here we are 30,000 feet up, and I feel the air of Macedonia. That means that the myth of Macedonia has become part of my red and white blood cells, not only in a spiritual sense, but also in a purely physiological way!"

But let's face it: Macedonian airspace is very small. If you fly into it from the north, via Serbia, you have to make your descent immediately, and if you come from Bulgaria, Greece or Albania, it's almost the same. An airspace that you can fly through in seven minutes. And when you consider that this land once stretched all the way to India . . . Now you can fly over it in seven minutes, or almost vault across it with a damn pole!

The airspace is small, Macedonia is small, and the number of its inhabitants is also small, fallen Alexander said to himself, but my idea for the Eighth Wonder of the World is great. Perhaps Macedonia has shrunk throughout its history, from Alexander the Great's time until today, so that this great idea of your concussed head can be realized, Alexander Simsar thought as the landing gear touched the runway of Skopje Airport. *Welcome to the capital of the Republic of Macedonia. The time is exactly 12:30.*

"Now we'll get the suitcases," Tsveta told him. "And we'll ask a taxei driver to take us straight to the church in the cemetery in V. Since it's Christmas, we can't go home until we've lit a candle in memory of the dead and for the wellbeing of the living."

The relationship between the dead and the living was one of the key themes of the building he had dreamed of, and Alexander felt the full weight of this central question while waiting for the suitcases and for their passports to be checked. He had been like this before, and now after his fall he could make intimate miracles happen, turning the dead into the living and making the living immortal! He could summon any person from Macedonian history, from any era, and enter an open dialogue with them. Sometimes he believed he could not only summon them but also hold them accountable, put them in the dock, and really take them apart for whatever reason, or for no reason at all. He could also hold all of Macedonian history in his hand—or did it just seem that way to him?—so that not even a bird could fly without his will.

"Exactly, my dear," he said to Tsveta. "We'll go from here straight to the cemetery. But bear in mind that, after my fall, I can't light a candle just for close relatives; the whole of Macedonia are now my relatives. If I take a candle and light it for all of Macedonia, I have two options: either I light a candle and say it represents the whole of Macedonia both below and above ground, or I take at least 300 candles and start lighting them for personalities that lived in this land, from the first Macedonian dynasty through to the present, and that means at least 3,000 years of history! We begin with the first Macedonian emperor Perdiccas, via his successors Archelaus, Philip, Alexander, Ptolemy, and Cleopatra, up to Roman times and the division of Macedonia into *Macedonia Prima* and *Macedonia Secunda* within the Roman Empire; after that came the eighteen Macedonian dynasties in Byzantium, plus all the saints, apostles, and martyrs who lived here and also mean something to me; there were even a significant number of Ottoman dignitaries who left their bones in Macedonian soil; later, from the fourteenth to the nineteenth century, there followed a long line of fresco painters, architects, wood carvers and stonemasons, writers and enlighteners, adventurers . . .

"Or even emperors—you can find them at every turn, wherever you look. Starting with Alexander, who literally created a new world; then Justinian I, who wanted to build eternity and shut it into the Hagia Sophia in Constantinople; and who do you take next? I'd have to light a candle for them all, and then for the whole Macedonian intelligentsia, scattered over the European metropolises and despairing of their homeland, and then for all the impoverished Macedonians through the centuries, for all the rich, for all the happy and unhappy, for all the despondent and deceived, for all the émigrés and refugees after the partition of Macedonia in the Balkan Wars (1912-1913), for the entire Macedonian diaspora . . . Oh, I must also light candles for the Macedonians who live all over Australia, Canada, the US, and Western Europe.

"But why only for the Macedonians? Since the fall, which I miraculously survived, I also have to light a Christmas candle for all the countries that worship not only Jesus, but Moses, Buddha, Mohammed, Brahma, Krishna, the Taoists . . . There was an international network of circumstances surrounding my fall, so I also have to light a candle for Germany and France, for all of Europe, for China, Africa, and Asia . . . India and Japan included, of course, and especially Russia, for which I feel an unparalleled, almost holy reverence . . ."

The taxei driver, who was stowing the luggage into the trunk, looked at Alexander and crossed himself three times. Tsveta held her husband by both hands and feared he might tip over right there on the asphalt of the Macedonian airport. If that happened, she'd pray to God that He lift them both up to heaven and turn them into nothing, because she believed that people actually were nothing, and only fancied during a particular phase of their earthly existence that they were something material. Suddenly she noticed that Alexander's gaze was petrified. She asked the driver if he had a bottle of water. Frightened by the fallen man's expression, he handed her a two-liter plastic bottle. Tsveta opened it and began to wet her husband's face, eyes, forehead, and hair. And, as if nothing had happened, the smile returned to his face. He licked his lips and said to the driver:

"I thank you for this splash of Macedonian water. It was so salutary. Please take us to Lychnidos—I mean Ohrid—but the route should pass through the ancient cities of Scupi, Stobi, and Herakleia; I want to feel like I'm traveling through ancient Macedonia. After Ohrid, please drive directly to the village cemetery in V. My wife will tell you the way. We want to light a candle there for our nearest and dearest!"

About twelve miles south of Skopje airport on the road to Ohrid, on the bridge over the Vardar, he greeted this river, which has not only flowed through Macedonia from Homer's time until today, but also flowed through his heart when he cried after his fall in Berlin; in those moments he thought all the rivers of the world flowed through his eyes, beginning with the Black River or Erigon near his home village, which then enters the Vardar, and in turn, runs like tears from his eyes and enters the Aegean Sea at Thessaloniki, the historical capital of Macedonia. After his fall, all rivers flowed through his eyes: the Danube and the Sava, the Rhine, the Spree and the Elbe, the Quiet Don, the Amu Darya and the Yangtze—so much did he love the rivers of this world.

"Damn and curse it, am I going mad?" he grumbled. "As if the rivers of the world were uncried tears, from my eyes that burn and thirst for beauty . . ."

Therefore you shouldn't be surprised by his delight,

unknown reader, when he saw that snow had fallen on his mother country. In the four historical cities on the way to V. he saw ancient Macedonia under snow for the first time. Justinian I (527-583), one the greatest emperors of all time, was born in the village of Taor (Tauresium), and after the catastrophic earthquake of 518 he built the famous city of Justiniana Prima in nearby Scupi. Macedonian snow on the Roman mosaics and the amphitheater were soothing like pure silver for fallen Alexander after his despair, and he wanted to shout with exultation, just as Justinian proclaimed to Solomon and the temple in Jerusalem when he set eyes on the imperishable edifice of the Hagia Sophia in Constantinople: "Solomon, I have defeated you!"

He wanted to shout out to his famous compatriot: "Justinian, come and bring Theodora, whom you found as a prostitute and made an empress. Come and attest that the only thing time does not change is the wafting of snow. It is the only connection with the vicissitudes of life. Buildings stand, but the snow falls on them just as our thoughts fall, melt, and disappear—unless they're made into stone. See me, emperor: I too have come for a building, but who knows if I'll be able to build it since the hour of my death is drawing menacingly close!"

In Stobi he saw the big baptistery under the snow. Snow also covered the first synagogue on European soil. *Everything is the same under the snow because the snow shows that God is the same for everyone*, Alexander thought, both before and after his fall. *The same is true of the sun, except I don't want to live in any country where it doesn't snow!*

Afterwards they continued on to the ancient Macedonian city of Herakleia Lynkestis, and there, too, everything was covered in snow. He and Tsveta sat down on one of the stone seats of the amphitheater, where the Mirinos family had sat eighteen and something centuries earlier—the stone seat still showed the names of its owners—while the driver in the car was telling himself he had never run into such a weirdo before, so educated and so kooky at the same time. Alexander had never seen Herakleia under snow. A deer with snow on its antlers sprang from the mosaics and ran toward him and Tsveta. He said to her:

"Look, a deer is coming to us from under the snow. That means we'll have a child: a stag out of stones in twenty-seven colors ! The mosaics of Herakleia are so beautiful, and in the rest of Europe nobody knows them. What sort of Europe is it that doesn't know itself?"

The snowflakes began to fall on their faces again. Tsveta followed him and said to herself: *My God, are we going to head for V. at last so we can light a candle in the cemetery before it gets dark?* He turned around, looked at her, kissed her through the snowflakes on her head, on her eyes, on her mouth, and told the waiting driver: "Take us to Lychnidos!"

Lychnidos—today Ohrid—was only seven miles from the cemetery in the village of V. *Is this really necessary?* Tsveta thought, exasperated, and pitied herself. *To drive to four ancient cities to see them under the snow—you must be at least 101 percent crazy!* But nothing could dissuade fallen Alexander from his obsession that he had to retrace that 2,000-year-long road[2] before lighting that candle. Fortunately, he contented himself with greeting Lake Ohrid through the car window and gazing up at the Galichitsa Range, where he was going to build the Eighth Wonder of the World.

In the ancient city of Lychnidos he became engrossed in pleasant conversation with a sculpture of the goddess Isis—which was discovered near the city gate in the second century AD—and touched her face. As he ran his fingertip over the forehead and eyes of the goddess, he looked up at the fortress and saw the medieval Macedonian tsar Samuel, who from there, as he lay dying, had to see 14,000 of his soldiers blinded and put in chains after the battle against the Byzantine emperor Basil II in 1014 AD; instead of 14,000 soldiers, Alexander thought in his frailty that he saw 1,400,000 blinded men shuffling away, never to return, a figure equal to the number of Macedonians left in present-day Macedonia if we ignore the two to three million in the diaspora. The image of Samuel and the soldiers disappeared again quickly because Alexander saw nothing was there—snow covered everything. He took a lump of snow, dropped it onto Tsveta's hot chest, and said in a whisper:

"I don't remember where I read that there is no gloom the snow cannot lighten. Our tribulations are past and we can continue to the cemetery of our nearest and dearest!"

When they arrived at the cemetery in V., the church was closed. Night had almost fallen and no soul could be seen. Fallen Alexander told the tired driver:

---

2 A reference to the Roman road Via Egnatia, which passed through Macedonia

"Wait just a little while we light a candle. In five minutes you can take us to our house and then your odyssey will be over!"

The wrought-iron gate of the cemetery in V. was famous far and wide. Crafted in 1673 by one of the best-known smiths in the Balkans, its central motif was the sixteen-ray Macedonian Sun, which here divides in two so that the master builders of V. can enter through the "Last Gate" like sons of the sun! Alexander pulled the latch and they went in, like late guests, among the dead souls of V.

Tsveta got out the candles she had bought in the Memorial Church in Berlin and lit two on her parents' grave and two on that of Alexander's parents. Alexander took a broom from the next grave and swept the snow off both. Tsveta laid a pot of plastic flowers before each of the stone crosses, as well as cookies brought from Germany, chocolate, candies, and a bottle of German wine. The Simsars' and Mikhailovs' family graves seemed to be amused when Tsveta kissed the photos under the glass discs on the white marble slabs. Alexander heard a sob that came from the depth of her heart; he went to her, tenderly took her hand, and dabbed her tears with a white handkerchief. They said farewell to the graves and headed back to the waiting taxei. Fallen Alexander took hold of the long iron latch again to close the famous Last Gate, and just as he was about to push it back into position he had to cling to the gate and gaze intently into the cemetery—he could hardly believe his eyes: tombs were opening, the dead hovered up eerily out of them, formed a long line, and headed toward him.

I cannot tell you for sure how he recognized the spirits because they were invisible, but he had fallen from a great height, so—whether you like it or not—you simply have to believe him.

First Alexander the Great came up to him and took him by the hand to stop him closing the iron gate. Initially the fallen man was thunderstruck and stared openmouthed; but he quickly remembered his urgent request and said straightway:

"Great emperor, you built a total of seventy-seven Alexandrias throughout the known world in your short lifetime. I beg you, please allow me to raise the Eighth Wonder of Galichitsa between the two lakes, right on the spot where your father Philip learned that your mother Olympias was pregnant!"

The great general and ruler answered him outright using the Old Macedonian word for *idiot*:

"You absolute *fereos*, what are you waiting for? Get started and build! Why are you seeking my permission? You are a mote in the eye of my eternity. Get thee gone, and do not appear before my eyes until the Eighth Wonder of the World is standing! Understand?"

Behind Alexander the Great, one by one, invisible to all except the fallen man, there came the *Diadochi* or successors of the emperor: after his death Antipater (323-319 BC), Ptolemy (319-279), and Antigonus the One-eyed (319-301), then King Pyrrhus (287-272) and Perseus the last Macedonian king (179-168), who was beheaded in Rome and only appeared as a head to our fallen Alexander in this dream. Next came the Roman Triumvir Mark Antony (42-31), the Byzantine emperor Justinian I mentioned above, and Anna Komnena of the Macedonian dynasty in Byzantium of the eleventh century AD, and after them came the great Ottoman architect Yusuf Sinan, of whom it is said that he implemented more buildings during his lifetime than anyone else. And then—wonder of wonders—they all held hands: the emperors and builders . . . and there was also a famous family of masons from V.!

Among them came the first master builders named Simsar, who are mentioned in a Byzantine document from the ninth century, beginning with Isidor Simsar, who said to him: *My child, I worked on the Second Temple in Jerusalem, just so you know,* and his son Avram Simsar said: *I worked at Masada Fortress on the west bank of the Dead Sea;* another, Mikhail Simsar, pulled on his other arm and complained: *I worked in Damascus eight hundred years before you, but nobody knows my name—so much for justice!* Another, named Arsen Simsar, revealed to him: *I am the one in your family who could make facades sing like beauties, from whose fine voices flowed the artful hand of V.'s masons, and I even worked in distant Vladivostok;* other unknown master builders came and held hands in the line, among them a man with a flowing beard down to his belt and a trowel in his hand, who raised his tool and even held the point up between Alexander's eyes: *My fallen child, think a little with your own head about all these unknown hands that washed themselves in the waters of Lake Ohrid; think about these eyes that wept at all the heights of the world raised through the ages, but no one knows or wants to acknowledge them; think about these hearts that suffered day and night for want of a bite of bread to be eaten in secret in a foreign land; there, from afar, we saw the forbidden face of Macedonia, this stricken land, where "even the stars whisper in Macedonian, but no one knows it." Think, Alexander, with your concussed head!*

"Naturally I think," Alexander called out as he held the iron gate of the cemetery in both hands, and in his mind the words began to break up into syllables—na-tu-ra-lly, I think, o Ma-ce-do-ni-a, my di-vi-ded and en-slaved home-land—and an orchestra of ancient, Byzantine, and Ottoman instruments began to play the separate syllables in his head. An orchestra! He could hardly believe it.

And a chain dance began, from Alexander the Great through the Roman emperors to the *Diadochi*; there were also three sultans among them; everyone started to dance along with the procession of his ancestors, and he grabbed Tsveta and gave her the handkerchief to lead the dance; Tsveta danced ahead, fallen Alexander next to her, and then came a long line of atheists, Jews, Christians, pagans, and Muslims, all intermingled; everyone was dancing the *Teshko*, the slow dance of farewell, at the iron gate of the cemetery in V. And he, Alexander, thought to himself: *the neurologist in Berlin was quite right—it's no mean feat to fall fifty-three-and-a-half meters*, and he danced and danced as if his legs were hardly touching the ground, he knelt and turned to the rhythm of the dance, and everyone else followed behind, until at a certain moment he called out to the orchestra:

"Stop the music. Silence, please!" and he spoke to the dancers:

"You have all come together not for my funeral, God

forbid, but on the occasion of my great return to life with the humble idea of the Eighth Wonder of the World. I ask you and beg you and implore you: should I build it or not?"

The line was very long. All those emperors, dignitaries, architects, and random supernumeraries from the world history of architecture flitted through his thoughts and appeared to him as ghosts emerging from the forgotten cemetery in that Balkan January night, and they whispered to him with one voice, or at least he thought they were whispering to him:

"Build the Eighth Wonder of the World and do not wait for anyone's permission. Begin immediately, child of God!"

Immediately after that "child of God," he heard the warm breath of Tsveta's voice, which entered his left ear, penetrated the atrium of his heart, passed through his soul, and out again through his throat; the word excited him so much that he shut the wrought-iron gate and started smothering his wife with kisses, from her face to her breasts, her hair, her eyes, and her left breast again; she just acknowledged with a surprised look that he wanted to do it then and there; now it was time for the right breast, and when fallen Alexander took both her nipples in his mouth at the same time and started getting loud, and when he pulled off her underpants and held her tongue between his teeth, the snow seemed to him like a mirror, and the nearness of the church gave her naked body a sacred dimension. He remembered the Romany fortune teller, who had come all the way from the Punjab in India and recommended to them several years earlier that they make love by the eastern wall of the closed church. This was not the eastern wall but the eastern side in general, and it had been ages since they last had sex standing up; he lifted her around the waist, and when his doppelganger (as he fondly called his penis) drove into her, he felt three emperors, three tsars, and 1,700 unknown master masons coming to orgasm at the same time as him, each within his own beloved wife, and he came inside Tsveta, who could delight him no end, as if he had been propelled to the very gates of heaven. But this was not the time for the Last Judgment; he was turned on and elated to the point of oblivion by the unexpected appearance of the spirits and their consent for the construction of the Eighth Wonder.

The tired driver waited patiently and could not have imagined—he wasn't crazy—that his passengers were mixing their juices out in the winter landscape. They returned to the car and Alexander showed the driver the way to the Simsars' house.

"This is it," he finally said. "Here are 200 marks for the ride and 200 marks for your patience in seeing me through the snows of ancient Macedonia!"

The village of V. lay in deep slumber. They entered the stone house with its seven rooms and three porches, built in 1823, and carried in the suitcases. Tsveta took the bedding out of her dowry chest, and they lay down to sleep on the cast-iron bed bought in Constantinople in the early nineteenth century; a peacock strutted on each side of the head. Alexander summoned sleep to fall on their eyes. Tsveta only needed a minute; he, too, was only a hair's breadth away from sinking into a deep sleep and even said to himself: *If I never wake up again, I won't be sad—I've had such a wonderful day!* Just at that moment, on the threshold of Hypnos's realm, as he was just a hair's breadth, a crumb, a speck away from sleep, the door opened a crack and the Envoy of the White Trade International and New World Order, Satanael Devil Shaitan Teufel Hudich Diabolus Gubernator Mundi appeared.

"Get up!"

Alexander slowly sat up, clambered over Tsveta's legs, and went to the door:

"Leave me alone, I've just come home!"

When he opened the door wide, he saw that a millstone had been set down in front of it, which weighed a good ton, if not more. The Envoy of the White Trade International and the New World Order spoke to him:

"Is it true that your mother gave birth to you in a water mill?"

"Yes, it is," Alexander said.

"So you always remember your birth and never forget what I've told you—that you mustn't build the Eighth Wonder of the World because it will produce a new world utopia—from now on you'll live with this millstone around your neck, and it will be with you whenever you move, work, sleep, read, think, and make love. Bend your head!"

Fallen Alexander bent forward and really did feel a heavy burden, as if the whole of Macedonian history was weighing down on his neck.

"If this millstone doesn't bring you to your senses, the White Trade International and the New World Order shall have no choice but to proceed to execution!"

The millstone hung around his neck now, but it was invisible to him and everyone else. The difference was that he alone felt its weight.

He snuggled up to Tsveta. Daylight broke and the roosters crowed in V.

To wear Macedonia like a millstone before you commence building the Eighth Wonder of the World isn't just a right, but a duty. One small effort for me, one giant leap for Macedonia, he said to himself. *If I can make love wearing a millstone of a ton and more around my neck, I don't think anyone can question the future of Macedonia and the Eighth Wonder of the World.*

3.3 Seconds

This is now the moment when the reader should pick up a pencil and take part in the construction of the Eighth Wonder of the World or the Cradle of the World, against whose realization the New World Order and the White Trade International represented by Mr. Satanael Devil Shaitan Teufel Hudich Diabolus Gubernator Mundi have already raised a monstrous accusation: that Alexander Simsar wanted to launch a new world utopia called Cradlism. In their own defense, and that of the fallen man, the reader can take a pencil and roughly calculate that the duration of the fall from the Memorial Church in Berlin is 3.3 seconds according to the basic principle of Newton's dynamics. To be exact, if one takes the height of the Berlin church as being 53.5 meters and Alexander's weight as 67 kilograms, and treats the drag of gravitation as the basis, one arrives at 3.3 seconds.

$$T= \sqrt{(53.5 \times 2/9.8)} = 3.3 \text{ sec.}$$

We can assume that the idea of the great Catalan architect Gaudí went through the head of our hero in these 3.3 seconds: that the architect is a person of synthesis and sees things as a whole before they are realized; he studies and connects elements according to their appearance, their relationship to each other, and their actual distances. And, to continue Gaudí's idea: form is only fourth on the list in architecture. Location comes first, proportion and place second, material and color third, and then form—fourth.

In terms of location, it will be in the Galichitsa Range that separates Lake Ohrid and Lake Prespa. Its origin dates back to the radial tectonic movements that occurred during the Tertiary, several million years ago. The highest part of the Galichitsa Range is a kind of plateau with four distinct crags rising above it: Magaro (7,395 feet), Lako Signoi (6,509 feet), Goga (5,698 feet), and Baba (4,934 feet). The Eighth Wonder of the World will be built on Baba Peak, because from there you can look out over both lakes. In addition to this view, which indisputably proves the link between Macedonia and infinity, since both border on themselves, there is another significant reason for the choice of Galichitsa: its universal, cultural-historical, and natural value. If we consider that Macedonia, with its more than 5,000 plant species, is a superpower of botanical biodiversity (Britain, for example, has less than 1,000 native plant species) then it's obvious!

The Galichitsa Range comprises nearly seventy percent of the total endemic population of trees and bushes, medicinal herbs, flowers, and indigenous woody plants. There is also the unique phenomenon that 1,200 species of moths have been recorded on this mythical mountain range and are preserved in the Natural History Museum in Skopje—although Macedonia's 9,928 square miles make it one of the smallest countries in the world. This natural topography will be an open challenge for the millions of visitors to the Eighth Wonder of the World who will immerse themselves in this ecological paradise for a few hours. But it's important to know that hunting butterflies and moths in Macedonia is strictly prohibited!

As for the second factor, the proportions, Alexander's ideas are roughly as follows: the Eighth Wonder of the World will be 3,280 feet long and 820 feet wide. Its 365 columns will be set evenly, eighteen feet apart, giving a total circumference of 6,437 feet. In the center there will be a cradle 328 feet long and 82 feet wide.

The third element is material and color. The exclusively white marble columns will come from the famous quarries at Prilep, mentioned by Alexander in his Berlin speech. The complex layers of marble have often aroused in him the idea that they were traces of God's conscience when He created the world, and now he would build the Eighth Wonder of the World from what remained of that divine purpose. You, dear reader, know that marble is created by the metamorphosis of organic limestone under high pressure in the course of the tremendous movements of rocks. These formed a body of marble many millions of years ago and made the grain size uniformly small, and this is the property that makes it possible to carve marble. Alexander believed it was no coincidence that Macedonia possesses immeasurable amounts of white marble, and that his own jolted mind had created this idea under enormous internal pressure.

Fourth and finally, the form. This will be ellipsoidal: a marble ellipse of harmoniously arranged columns around the wooden ellipse of the cradle on taut steel wires. According to his estimates, 80,016 feet of high-quality steel wire (Type 3650) will be required—forged, heat-stretched, and normalized. Steel wires will run to the cradle from every column. An elliptical ring of special steel (Type 561) will be mounted around the edges of the cradle, as a resonator, which the wires will pass through, and it will be connected to the cradle by steel grooves. This will create a resonance box with projectable acoustics: the Cradle of the World will serve as a harp of eternity to lull the whole world to sleep. Seen from far above, it will look as if the columns are swaying. Actually the cradle will rock in the interplay of the winds that blow from the Black Sea, the Mediterranean, and the Atlantic, and the lullabies of all the known and unknown languages of the world will sound there day and night, "twenty-four seven." The arrangement will be so impressive that the whole planet will sometimes wish it could fall asleep and never wake up again.

As you know, an idea that is not dangerous cannot be called an idea at all. The idea of the Eighth Wonder of the World began to take shape with dangerous, even fatal speed, according to his drawings. Indeed, this building so innocently committed to paper, as indescribable and unreal as a still life of his jolted mind, became a reality not in 3.3 seconds—the duration of his fall—but in a fraction of a second!

An unprecedented sight, invisible to the ordinary human eye, opened up before him, though we may forgive him because of his spectacular fall: an almost innumerable host of workers were toiling and sweating, a good 15–20,000 men of different ancestry and color—white, black, yellow, and red.

He wandered invisible between them, while the ground in the Macedonian marble gaped wide, and from it they pried and heaved layers of marble, cut them with stone saws, and milled the columns according to his instructions. "It can't be!" the fallen man marveled. "All the countries that were once part of Alexander the Great's Macedonian empire are represented here! This makes me so incredibly happy."

But he immediately felt a twinge and his conscience began to trouble him. If the marble from Macedonia and all over the world was a remnant of divine purpose, and if his conscience contained even a speck of dust of that divine purpose, he would have to ask himself at the same time who these unknown stone-crafters were that were shaping the 365 columns for the Eighth Wonder of the World: humans or gods?

Out of the blue, a thought thundered into his concussed brain as he watched them—that of Xenophanes of Colophon, one of the pre-Socratics from the sixth century BC:

One god: greatest among gods and humans,
dissimilar from mortals in body and in thought.
All of him sees, all thinks, all hears.
But without exertion,
he shakes everything with the workings of his mind.
Remaining always in the same place, unmoving,
it is not fitting for him to travel here and there.

What is the "all" that Xenophanes contemplates? Can the construction of the Eighth Wonder of the World be a substitute for the whole that rises above death?

He asked himself that question, and he also gave the answer: *Yes, it can. Certainly it can, everything is possible. Absolutely possible. You can see 20–30,000 strangers using cranes and levers to break the marble, laying all the 365 columns, 53.5 meters long, side by side, and then disappearing again as if nothing had happened. Each column consists of five drum-shaped sections; the first four are ten meters long, the fifth 13.5 meters, and iron bars protrude from each section to connect them together. In other words, they are now ready to be transported, and they number five times 365 columns, or 1,825 sections.*

Yes, it can, because it is an invaluable idea realized with remarkable swiftness, he thought, *with the speed of light even, since the earth itself—every person alive, or who lived and then died—feels a need for this idea, which was being turned into an edifice before his very eyes.*

There were very few ideas in the world that were turned into a structure, like the Eighth Wonder of the World, which was now being built, thank God. And it was taking shape in every single person, regardless of their religious and national affiliation, their age, and their material, social, economic, and political circumstances; it was simply being built, in his native Macedonia, in a place chosen by him, and it would become a reality no one could deny. Fallen Alexander Simsar even wanted to address the volunteer workers from everywhere with a short speech to express his gratitude for their altruistic efforts of breaking and cutting the marble and trimming the columns. But no sooner had he opened his mouth and arranged his thoughts: *Brothers and sisters, ladies and gentlemen, representatives of peoples far and wide, humiliated and insulted, and others . . .* than everything disappeared around him. They were gone—the workers, the lifting devices, and the stone saws; deathly silence reigned in the marble quarry. There really was no one there anymore. The columns lay stacked in the open, waiting to be transported to the summit of the Galichitsa Range.

All right, people come and go, there are more people everywhere, fallen Alexander consoled himself, *but marble columns are rare. These pillars are invaluable now, as the basic structural element of the planned wonder of the world.*

He grasped at his heart because it still hurt him deeply that the men had all left without him having a chance to greet them. As soon as he raised his moping head from the road, where the former Via Egnatia ran from Constantinople to Salonika and on to Rome, he saw no fewer than 750 trucks, all of them in motion. He counted every single one of them. Each truck weighed about twenty tons, and all of them were making for Baba Peak in the Galichitsa Range. It struck him as rather odd that the trucks all had different number plates and country symbols: there were German, French, Serbian, Bulgarian, Greek, Dutch, and Belgian trucks, even Chinese and Russian ones, and he felt a momentary pang of despair that was expressed in sweat on his forehead. *It's a sovereign Macedonian idea after all, or rather my own, and I don't know who bade all these trucks come that belong to other states,* he thought. But his universalistic spirit told him in his heart that a large number of European and non-European countries might have been informed by a spy ring after his speech in Berlin—countries that might have an interest in participating in the construction of the Eighth

Wonder of the World through material and financial support or providing a fleet of trucks.

That comforted him a little at first, but soon he was seized by a wave of indignation: how could it be that all those powerful states were only contributing trucks? Couldn't they have provided helicopters, or special cargo aircraft to load and transfer the columns to their destination in no time?

But then fallen Alexander checked himself: Where would such huge planes, heavily loaded, land and then take off again? And so he reconciled himself with the image of the trucks being filled one after the other: seventy forklifts raised the columns and loaded them onto the trucks, which then drove off and climbed the mythical mountain between the two lakes, where the establishment of the Eighth Wonder of the World would change the course of human history because, when the names of the saviors and the great murderers of people were hewn in stone once and for all, they'd begin to revitalize the currents of humanity. They'd act as a new alphabet of humanism, which every day is dying in you, me, and all of us!

The unidentifiable representatives of the human species, the forklifts, and the column-laden trucks set off toward the Galichitsa Range, where his childhood dream would take shape. He was alone again. There were yawning gaps in the big body of marble, and blue water gushed from the wounded bowels of the earth. He saw himself naked in the mirrors of its marble wounds. He began to pat down his body, from his shoulders over his chest, his legs . . . yes, he was completely naked in the dark Macedonian night, as stark naked as when he was born. Only the marble body of the earth shimmered white before him. And he began to cry out into the night: "O white marble mother, where have you led me in this white gloom? Come and free me, dear mother! A heavy weight that I carried in the depths of my heart, now a core of black marble, has come dangerously loose."

And at his call, something quite unbelievable occurred before this forlorn, naked man, our fallen Alexander: from the nightly marble quarry, which looked as if all the secrets of divine purpose had been wrenched from the Macedonian soil, costumes began to appear to him, one after another, from ancient to Roman, Byzantine and Ottoman dress, to the clothes of today's postmodern, postmortem Macedonia.

First, long white woolen underpants appeared—leggings of white cloth—that jiggled toward him in the air and then hung in front of his face. Stunned, he took them in his hands, pulled them on, and realized he was still whole. He felt his heart and touched his cock, the two organs that according to Aristotle have a life of their own, and said to himself: Holy moly, I'm still alive and in one piece!

Then an old-fashioned cloth of fine wool went fluttering through the night; it was richly embroidered with birds, flowers, angels, and endless roads. After that, one piece of clothing after another came flying up to him: a double-breasted vest with silver and gold thread, a pair of baggy Turkish-style trousers, an undershirt with a sleeveless vest and a colorfully striped woolen sash. As if that was not enough, then came long white knitted socks with garters, and peasant shoes with leather straps. All of this came flying up to him bit by bit, and he donned this Balkan folk costume piece by piece. He patted his legs and felt his arms to see whether the clothes that had appeared out of nowhere were on properly, or perhaps back to front, and whether they really existed, since the Eighth Wonder of the World was under construction: *From now on everything is possible,* fallen Alexander said to himself. *It's even possible that I die and don't know that I've died, or that I'm already dead and think I'm alive.*

The blue water that shone in his eyes and the white marble wounds in the black earth were suddenly cut by a purple flash. Swiftly, as if by magic, a purple cloak flew toward him, fell right on his shoulders, and draped itself around them. The floor-length purple cape recalled one that a Celtic Druid once made for Alexander the Great; our fallen hero had read that the Celts reached the Balkans before Alexander the Great set out on his long journey to India.

Strange . . . All this reminded him strongly of the clothes of a dead man. Would he be buried in this gaping marble grave, clad in the darkness of eternity, with the idea that he had outfitted the centuries of his memory like the men of Macedonia had dressed from Alexander the Great to his day?

No, definitely not!

A white horse appeared before him with a saddle and jingling bells, with reins and spurs. He caressed this gift horse with trembling fingers; it whinnied and waited almost impatiently for the rider, who no longer knew whether he was dead or alive, naked or clothed, whether he was buried or already risen, whether he was forgotten and moldering in the past, or would soon stride into the future.

An invisible hand lifted him into the saddle, in his archaic clothing, and the steed rose up into the air as it does in all the myths between the Himalayas and Macedonia in at least 300 different languages—for a horse in a dream that cannot fly is no proper horse!

There is a beautiful expression in Macedonian: *The wind carries him on a white horse.* The wind streams that arise from the gales between the Black Sea and the Mediterranean blew him into the black night on his white mount, and he thought to himself: *If all this is true, it must be a big lie. He* imagined he was still falling from the scaffolding of the church in Berlin, and he worried that questions crucial for the construction of the Cradle of the World had yet to be resolved:

1. The statics of the structure, the depth of the foundations, and the ratio of the distance between the columns must be calculated.

2. The whole ritual of casting the foundations and the preparatory digging would have to be done from the eastern side and be connected with the sprinkling of holy water from the sacred sites of different religions. Should one sacrifice rams, lambs, and roosters, as practiced in many traditions of the world? He personally rejected this, especially since no trace of blood should compromise the purity of his aspired structure, and that ruled out the shedding of animal and human blood.

3. Five tons of steel wire, 0.78 inches thick and a total of 80,016 feet in length, were needed to connect the cradle with

the columns, and the tension would create a perpetual rocking effect—something unique in the world of architecture, and in general!

4. Electricity and water must be supplied, and a paved road constructed that would connect the Eighth Wonder of the World via existing roads with the highways of Europe and beyond. Some infrastructure already existed in the vicinity of Ohrid (also known as "the ancient mystery," the "Venice of the Balkans," and the "Slavic Jerusalem").

5. It might be necessary to build a lift or funicular similar to that in Lisbon designed by Gustave Eiffel, the creator of the Eiffel Tower in Paris, so that pilgrims from all over the world could ride up to the Cradle of the World in the Galichitsa Range from the nearest point on the Ohrid road.

6. The recruitment of qualified stonemasons to craft the columns and carve the names of the Savior Children and Murderer Children—in all possible languages of the world, of course—would have to be arranged in a definite order by him as initiator of the project.

7. The lighting system, i.e., the number of spotlights that would need to be set up to illuminate the Cradle of the World from different angles and make it attractive for night visits.

8. The sound system that would reproduce the lullabies of the peoples of the world, which would have to be recorded for the Eighth Wonder of the World in the name of humanism.

9. Official government approval—although permission had already been obtained from Moses, Jesus, Buddha, Mohammed, and Shiva!

10. The open threat of the Envoy of the New World Order, Satanael Devil Shaitan Teufel Hudich Diabolus Gubernator Mundi. This critical and perhaps even lethal factor must not be forgotten . . .

No sooner had he pronounced that name than Alexander felt the millstone of a ton and more around his neck, but he let the white horse carry him away in the wind. When he opened his eyes again, he saw he was at the summit of the Galichitsa Range and, believe it or not, there he saw the columns! All 365 of them were already up on the mountain and secured; they looked like giant stalks that had grown out of the earth and were striving skywards. He admired this forest of vertical columns, arranged in an ellipse, that he had dreamed of all his life, and, just like in his design, a steel wire ran from every column to the central circle and swung gently in the air; only that inner space was still empty. Everything else stood proudly, as if 81,322 laborers had toiled there, as they had at the temple complex in Karnak, according to an ancient Egyptian papyrus from 1150 BC. Only the cradle was still missing. Where was the Cradle of the World and who would bring it here?

He looked up at the sky and saw it as in a picture from the Yiddish legends hidden in the farthest corner of his unhinged memory: as a curtain that God had drawn shut so He wouldn't see the happenings on earth. The curtain was closed. *God isn't there*, Alexander said to himself. *I'm sure He has more important things to do than waste his time with a birdbrained Icarus and his pipe dream of building an eighth wonder of the world.*

But that's not how it was: behold, God's curtain opened

a little and a head that resembled that of his father, Philip, peered out . . . and disappeared again.

"Father, Father!" Alexander cried. "Father, please come down and talk to your fallen son one last time. I saw you up in the scaffolding of the Memorial Church in Berlin and I remember everything you told me, and it all came about of its own accord, without my intervention. It seems I'm incapable of doing anything myself, and I feel I'm even ruining what little I've done!"

Incredible as it seems, a man appeared in the place where the sky or the curtain of God had opened, and started to climb. He was wearing a tradesman's smock over his long white shirt, and a plumb bob dangled from his belt together with a spirit level and an adze. He clambered down from the sky, stopped briefly when he reached the top of the columns, and then went from one to another. He stretched the plumb line and dropped the bob, measured the columns' position with the spirit level, tapped them with the adze, and listened to the strange sound that echoed all over the mountain and was lost in the endlessness. Fallen Alexander followed his movements from below, bawling like a child, and repeated: *Father, my Heavenly Father, hallowed be thy name, make sure this house, which I have dreamed of all my life, will stand the test of time—a house I saw for the first time at your funeral, that I also saw during my fall, and have now found ready and built, just like you said to me in Berlin, the night before my fall. Please now tell me what kind of wood the Cradle of the World should be made of, where I can find that tree, how I should fell it, and how I make the cradle.*

After checking all the marble columns that were connected to the steel column on the eastern side, his father let himself slide down from heaven to earth, like God's messenger. He arranged the tools on his belt, sat down, and spoke to his son:

"Sit down opposite and I'll tell you everything. You've not done anything wrong so far: the height is adjusted, the depth of the foundations is fine, and the statics are correct."

"And the cradle?"

"Tell me, dear son: do you know where the most beautiful cradles and the most beautiful coffins in the world are made?"

"No."

"The most beautiful cradles and coffins in the world are made in Salonika, the heart and historical capital of geographical, economic, political, spiritual, and above all natural Macedonia."

"Why Salonika, exactly?" his son asked.

The father answered as follows:

"For the last few thousand years, Thessaloniki—or Salonika, Solun, etc.—was the most cosmopolitan city in the Balkans. Not only Macedonian barbarians and ancient Greeks were born and buried there, but in the following centuries also the subjects of the Roman and Byzantine empires: Slavs, Normans, Venetians, and of course the Jews, without whose bones, dreams, and houses the history of the city would be unthinkable; and of course the Armenians, and it's said that the Salonika cherry trees are so splendidly white in blossom because they're watered by Armenian tears; and of course there is also the Ottoman and Turkish heritage of the city, and then the French, German, Russian, English, and finally American presence, and they all co-wrote the tumultuous history of the city, so that a Greek scholar said last century: In Salonika even the air, the water, the stones, and the very trees are of multi-ethnic origin!

"Since we've mentioned trees, and the tree contains the whole secret of crafting the cradles and coffins, let's look at some of the essentials: which tree, from which botanical area and height above sea level, which variety and subspecies, how old the tree should be, what time of year it should be felled, and what temperature the tree should be stored at so that it becomes part of the mystery preserved for centuries among the multiethnic carpenters of that city. The art of cradle- and coffin-making has flourished here to such a degree that there's almost no one who hasn't already spoken the Macedonian proverb in their own language: 'You weren't born if you weren't rocked in a Salonikan cradle, and you're not properly dead if you didn't leave in a Salonikan coffin!'

"But let's leave aside the coffins so that this story will have an end. We're only interested in the cradle now.

"A Salonikan cradle is made of cherry wood. The tree must be between twelve and twenty-four years old. The painful act of its felling is carried out in the spring, on a night with a crescent moon, just when the first glorious white petals fall and the fruit emerge in their place as tiny dots or 'cherry newborns.' The felling has been virtually unchanged for centuries: the master craftsman who makes the cradle comes to the earmarked tree in person with his axee and begins the ritual of swinging and chopping along a groove carved in the bark with a small knife. At every third blow, he speaks a word, until he finally arrives at the sacred number of 101, so that the newborn will live to be at least 101.

"The story of the hundred-and-first word in the crafting of the Salonikan cradles is one of the most interesting in the culture of birth and infancy worldwide. It's passed on from father to son, from mother to daughter, from brother to brother, from sister to sister, from man to woman and woman to man, from generation to generation. Originally, many centuries ago, the 101 words were all in Old Macedonian, the language of Alexander the Great. After his departure from Macedonia to conquer the world as far east as India, and especially after the fall of his empire, words from the languages of all new conquerors and new slaves found their way into the 101 words. Since the craft of cradle-making (we're leaving aside the coffins) had to be preserved in the 101 words in the face of ever newer influences—people are still born and die—by the late nineteenth or early twentieth century only three words of Old Macedonian remained in the 3,000-year-old ritual of cherry-tree felling for cradle-making because words were successively added from other languages: Persian, Hebrew, Ancient Greek, Latin, Phoenician, Aramaic, Hunnic, Gothic, Norman, Scythian, Old Slavic, Tatar, Turkish, Armenian, Aromanian . . . and not to forget Ladino, the language of the Spanish Sephardic Jews, who immigrated here in great numbers in the fifteenth century after the expulsion; and not to forget the more recent conquerors and armies, who came with their languages and still speak them today: French, English, German, Italian, Russian . . .

"But back to the master craftsman and the felling of the tree. Picking up his perfectly sharpened axe, he swings three times without striking, and then begins to utter the ritual, warm words that every newborn is greeted with, regardless of ethnicity, language, religion, race or color, because the birth of every child brings joy to the heart and an indescribable sparkle to the eyes.

"A spring night, a crescent moon: the craftsman raises his axee and delivers the first blow, then another, and a third; the cherry tree begins to cry, white petals and the first embryonic fruits rain down, and he speaks the words in succession:

Three nicks and three words in Old Macedonian:
Asini nimia sila
(O glowing thirst of love)

Three nicks and three words in Ancient Greek:
Katarhazi omnia tai
(May the spirit of your body bloom)

Three nicks and three words in Hebrew:
Inse telea hamram
(May the star on your forehead be your world)

Three nicks and three words in Persian:
Elamit ahura mazda

(May the great God be with you)

Three nicks and three words in Latin:
Diura acta populi
(May the people know you are born)

Three nicks and three words in Aramaic:
Marani asra sizomsa
(May love lend you wings)

Three nicks and three words in Old Slavic:
Dzyalo slontse slovo
(May the sun be your guide)

Three nicks and three words . . .

". . . and so on until the hundred and first word in all the languages mentioned, which the master craftsman speaks as he ritually fells the cherry tree. One of the most famous makers of Salonikan cradles, Isidor Sirak, came from Krontselevo, a Macedonian village in the hills from where you can see the famous waterfalls of Voden (in Greek: Edessa); today it bears the name Kerasia, 'cherry village,' which is fitting since the hillsides bear thousands of the most beautiful cherry trees in Europe. According to Sirak's reminiscences, the most recent addition to the 101 words occurred in the fifteenth century, when three words of Ladino were included—not counting the addition in the nineteenth century of one word of French, English, German, Italian, and Russian.

"According to the story passed down by his son Bogomil, Isidor Sirak was even called to the Sublime Porte at the beginning of the twentieth century after the last Ottoman sultan, Abdülhamid II, had admired a Salonikan cradle from Sirak's workshop. The sultan rewarded the master with handsome gifts and said to him: 'I heard as a child that 101 words in many languages are uttered when felling the cherry tree. Can you find room for three words of Turkish to be spoken last, just before the fall of the tree and the spell for the newborn baby to be rocked in the cradle in future?' Sirak thought for a moment and answered the sultan: 'Certainly, Your Highness. Which words?'

"And from that moment to this day, the Salonikan master cradle-makers pronounce the Turkish words right at the end:

Bu yalan dünyada tek gerçek sensin!
(Only you are the truth in this false world!)

"Then the time has come: one last turn and swing of the axe, one last word, and the cherry tree falls in the spring night. White blossoms like a gift from the Lord and the little fruits like tears of God cover the face of the craftsman and the body of the tree. The trunk is carried to the workshop and, covered with petals, it lies there for nine months, as long as a child lies in the womb of its mother. After the ninth month, the bark is removed and long saws are used to cut the wood into wafer-thin boards, which are then carved with all manner of boons and blessings: flowers, trees, fruits, mountains, rivers, and lakes; the bed for the newborn is hollowed out like an inverted vault of heaven, two falcons are carved at the foot end to guard its fortunes, and a rainbow at the head. Finally, the wood is painted with masterfully executed semicircles, with the same paints that are used for frescoes; they last for centuries and their formulation is a secret passed on from generation to generation.

"All of them were born and rocked in the bottomless well of Salonikan history, in such cradles and with such words: Macedonian generals, Homer's rhapsodists, Roman consuls and Christian apostles, Byzantine emperors and Jewish philosophers, as well as bards and dancers, traders and murderers, and the victims and heroes of all the peoples who left their mark on the city, where lullabies were sung in over 200 languages. Yes, my son, in that very city!"

Alexander's father got up, looked into the forest of columns, and saw the empty space of the cradle. Then he glanced at Lake Ohrid and Lake Prespa, as if he were looking into the eyes of his fallen son who had been crying in torrents, and asked him:

"My son, I forgot to ask, may God forgive me: do you have any children?"

"Tsveta is pregnant, we're expecting a child!"

Then his father, Philip Simsar, went to the same eastern column from which he had descended and began to climb up, as light as a feather, to the top, and from there he went to the same gap in God's heavenly curtain, which again opened a crack to let him in. Alexander's eyes followed him until the last moment when the curtain closed, and when his gaze sank back to the building . . . what did he see? An unimaginable miracle: a huge Salonikan cradle of cherry wood was hanging there on the tensioned steel wires just like in his drawings—one hundred meters long and twenty-five meters wide.

And what did the cradle do? It rocked in the breezes between the Black Sea and the Mediterranean!

Imagine the expectant mother, Tsveta Mikhailova, who now came rushing up to the cradle with the rainbow carved at the head and two falcons at the foot, tenderly embraced it and took it into her soul, her heart, her womb, and then kissed the eyes of her unborn child and its brow bedewed with white cherry blossoms!

Imagine the father too, Alexander Simsar, the Great or the Fallen, with his sick head, from which the whole world that existed before him and would prevail after him now unraveled like a ball of black wool. The building and the child, for which they had been waiting for centuries, were at the center of all his thoughts. Imagine the fraction of a second when the secret treasure chambers of Salonika's multiethnic life sprang open, that which Greek chauvinism intended to suppress when it occupied that cosmopolitan city with its army in the infamous partition of Macedonia. Alexander's fall-injured brain center pulsated with the idea of one of the most powerful modern minds of twentieth-century Greece, Elias Petropoulos, the exiled living legend, who said that Salonika hadn't been Greek even for two minutes in the 2,000 years of its history.

Alexander imagined the Cradle of the World, made by master

cradle-maker Bogomil Sirak, setting off from 12 Theotokos (Mother of Good) Street to fly over Macedonia one last time before his triumphant return to embrace the Vardar River that flows into the Aegean, to pass over the Shara and Galichitsa ranges to Ohrid and Lake Prespa, and to greet Bezbog Peak in the Pirin range; without forgetting the Black River, the glacial lakes called "Pelister Eyes," Mount Kaymakchalan and the peak Solunska Glava. Along the way were also Mount Vicho, the stone bridge over the Vardar in Skopje, the graves of his and Tsveta's parents, medieval churches and monasteries, the mosques, madrassas, caravanserais, and dervish monasteries from the Ottoman era, as well as the synagogues, Roman amphitheaters, Greek orchestras, and ancient Macedonian necropolises—all those structures from all those times that even a healthy mind cannot remember, let alone a mush-brain like his after the fall to the hard Berlin sidewalk.

He turned around and saw Tsveta, her face pressed against the rainbow of the Salonikan cradle, and he saw her beautiful lips move and heard her sing the longest lullaby in the world: a silent song without words. There, beneath the rainbow of the Salonikan cradle, he nestled his face next to hers. Utter silence reigned on the summit of the Galichitsa Range—there was no one but them and the Eighth Wonder of the World. He saw her and his lips moving, without speaking a single word; he thought of the craftsman who felled the cherry tree and what he must have been thinking of when he pronounced the hundred and first word so as to make this cradle; he saw the tree fall over her, and in the rhythm of the movement of her lips, fallen Alexander heard the white blossoms raining down like words that no one else could hear except him. Petals fall all over the world, just as the words in every language of the world irretrievably fall everywhere, but no one has asked themselves where the solemn words go that are spoken at birth, in love, and at death—the only points that connect humanity.

And what happened after the word "humanity" shot through his jolted mind at the speed of light?

Something happened that was simple and at the same time difficult. For the first time, he saw the Eighth Wonder of the World as a whole: the columns stood fast, as if they had been rooted in the earth for all eternity; the steel wires ran through the cherry-wood Cradle of the World so neatly as if God Himself had sewed them with the needle of eternity; and the cradle rocked as if it was destined to herald a new era in world history after his fall.

The image of an ancient Macedonian custom arose in his shaken mind, a tradition that Macedonian master builders spread throughout the world for centuries: the topping-out ceremony called *vikanye na chatiya* or "shouting on the roof." When the fabric of a building is complete, the master craftsman climbs up to the highest point and gives a short speech; well-wishers who want to donate to the building then come with gifts that are announced with a shout from the roof so that the consecration is heard from afar and the building is blessed both for eternity and in the here and now.

And what did he see when he looked around?

A mass of people and shadows were moving toward the

base of the Eighth Wonder of the World from all sides of the Galichitsa Range; all the languages of the world could be heard and they merged into a din, a confusion of words like with the Tower of Babel, except that the structure here was complete. He thought he saw thousands upon millions of unknown faces; such crowds arose, such a tremendous throng, that he said to himself: *These hordes will destroy the building and my lifelong dream, just when my wife has come to have our child here . . .*

Suddenly everything calmed down, and silence returned on earth and in heaven.

A shadow—was it a person or a creature?—scaled the eastern steel column, and he thought it would have to be his father again, who had forgotten to tell him something. The shadow stopped at the top of the column as if to initiate a "roof shouting" ceremony; he raised his hands to the sky, but he didn't call out.

Fallen Alexander looked up to the curtain of the sky that God had drawn shut so as not to see anything, and—what do you know—it opened a little. He heard a voice like a voiceover, as loud as a megaphone and in Macedonian, but lamenting and somewhat offstage: the chief of the Indian delegation wanted to greet the Eighth Wonder—the Cradle of the World in Macedonia.

Alexander was stupefied, but he soon consoled himself again: *Blood is thicker than water, after all. India is our biggest relative. It's not by chance that Alexander went all the way to India. It's no coincidence that Indian legends call him "the Two-Horned One who touched the extremes between East and West."*

The Indian exclaimed:

"In the name of all the languages, cultures, and civilizations that no longer exist, we give the head of this house and his family a shirt from the Punjab with a holy cow embroidered by 2,000 hands. We bring 3,000 names of Savior Children and 7,000 names of Murderer Children that we want to carve into the columns of the Eighth Wonder of the World, the Cradle of the World. We accept the idea of the new world utopia, cradlism, because it sounds very enticing: the word for cradle in Hindi, for example, is *jhula*, so we have jhulism. Or *palna*—palnism."

After that, the head of the Chinese delegation was announced from the same opening in God's curtain. Fallen Alexander began to wonder and mumbled to himself: *I understood the Indian representative more or less, but how is it going to work with Chinese?* After climbing to the top of the Eighth Wonder of the World, the Chinese delegate first bowed to the sky and then looked down directly into the eyes of the worried architect. One thing should be clear from the outset: according to legend, Chinese goddess Nugua needed 36,500 blocks of stone to build the heavens. *Yes, Nugua in legend and me in the real world—if that same basic number isn't a Chinese-Macedonian invention!*

"China welcomes the idea of raising the Cradle of the World in Macedonia and presents the fallen architect *(China knows that I fell!)* a porcelain vase *(it's sure to fall and break!)* with 27,000 details from 6,000 years of Chinese civilization, from Taoism to this day. We propose a reduced number of 9,000 Savior and 8,000 Murderer Children to be carved into the columns. The idea of cradlism, which would be called noism in Chinese, does not contradict our view of the world in any way. Long live the cradle!"

Next came the head of the Japanese delegation, who, in the spirit of martial arts, immediately performed a backwards somersault in the air and landed neatly on his feet. He then announced that he had dedicated a three-line haiku to the construction, and proceeded to declaim:

A pale star of wax
Yearning that cuts the morning
In rapture profound

Not only did he have nothing against the idea of cradle and cradlism—that would be *yurikago*, in Japanese, and consequently yurikagism—but he declared that he would kill himself right there, at the highest point, out of shame that no living person from the Land of the Rising Sun had thought of building this edifice, but that it was born in the mind of a fallen Macedonian. And, true to his word, he flung himself headfirst off the column, but not before stabbing himself in the belly on both sides with a sharp Japanese knife. Alexander was so shaken by the sight that he almost died of fear a second time, but he had no time to react. His distorted perception, which had been diagnosed in the Augusta Victoria Hospital in Berlin, meant that everything unfolded for him at a rapid pace.

After that, the envoy of the island states between the Indian and Pacific Oceans and all the countries of Indochina spoke:

"Indochina, the Philippines, Indonesia, and New Guinea have long been waiting for this idea because we are all too well-acquainted with carnage, famine, and fire; we know how it destroys the life people have dreamed of, and how terror between human beings prevents us from believing in the dignity of every individual. We give the Eighth Wonder of the World and its builder a magical cult object: a sheath decorated with the horns of a Borneo bull, which hides the penis of the wearer and is tied with a string around his neck when he appears in public. To his wife, we give magnificent earrings of Philippine turtle shell in memory of Alexander Simsar's visit to the world's largest Buddhist temple complex, Borobudur, in his years with the German firm World Construction. The cradle and cradlism? We say yes, unreservedly! We have many languages, but in Vietnamese it is *noi* and noism. If global capitalism continues to fuel poverty, noism will re-establish order tomorrow, and there is bound to be bloodshed."

Finally, he mentioned the number of Savior Children and Murderer Children.

Fallen Alexander wondered how he could instantly understand all these languages and all the numbers cited by the representatives from different countries. How could he manage all this in his mind, which, as we know, was in such a scrambled state? But it went on like this, without end. Sometimes the curtain in the sky opened, sometimes it closed; sometimes a person came out, sometimes another went in. *Has the door to infinity opened in my injured head?* he wondered, as this version of the ancient Macedonian "roof shouting" custom continued.

Now the head of the Saudi delegation and representative of the Arab countries spoke:

"We know how much the creator of the Eighth Wonder of the World is inspired by the buildings throughout the Arab world," he said. "Therefore, here in Macedonia, we present a piece of the black stone that fell to earth several centuries ago in Wabar, in the Rub' al-Khali desert in Saudi Arabia. As for the Cradle of the World or cradlism, we have nothing against this utopia, since it threatens no one. In Arabic it is *mahd*, and thus mahdism. A very appropriate name! When you say *Mahd al-Hadara* in Arabic, the cradle of world civilization, your soul and body are enlightened. Long live the building of Iskender— our name for Alexander in Arabic!"

Finally he mentioned the number of Savior Children and Murderer Children, but our hero was unable to take in anything anymore: neither languages nor gifts nor numbers nor countries nor people. He stared up at God's curtain and saw Indra, son of the Stone Sky in Indo-Iranian mythology, breaking the stone of the sky with a hammer, and rain began to pelt down as if the whole of world history would collapse on his head, although he knew that history does not run according to the rhythm of individuals' lives, neither before nor after the fall. And still the shouters, the gifts, and the words all seemed to strike him on the head, like one blow after another.

The representative of Russia called out:

"I bring an icon painted by Andrei Rublev, which shows the Veil of Veronica. The number of Savior Children: 112. Murderer Children: 2,700. We accept the utopia of the cradle, from *kolybel* we have kolybelism. May kolybelism reign on earth tomorrow!"

A guest from the African continent arrived with a wonderful gift: a mask from the Limpopo River proving that Africa and Macedonia are cousins when it comes to using gold to make death masks.

"The number of saviors is unknown—there are none— and the number of murderers is also impossible to establish," the delegate said. "We find the cradle quite a success, and cradlism has a secure future in African civilization, which for centuries has been exposed to the terror of global capitalism."

Then it was the turn of a Latin American, who brought with him an extraordinary gift: a stone from Machu Picchu in Peru, from the Inca civilization's mysterious city of Intihuatana, which served as a timekeeping device—it cast a shadow on columns that were danced around by *mamaconas*, young devotees of the sun god. The number of saviors had to be counted from all the countries, the guest from Latin America said, as did the number of murderers, but the figures would be forwarded as soon as possible.

"Cradle is *cuna*, and the new utopia—cunism—has been received with applause. Long live cunism!"

Indra's hammer blow had left the sky wide open, and now the "shouting on the roof" morphed into a veritable rumbling of stones and words that crashed down on Alexander's poor head. It rained words and gifts, as if world history had turned into a hailstorm of stones, and he could no longer tell who was climbing up to "shout from the roof" of the Eighth Wonder of the World. He saw a unit of "Blue Helmets" approaching in United Nations uniforms—they would keep order the way UN Peacekeepers do. It was high time because the countless representatives of delegations large and small were vying to climb the column and announce their gift to the builder of the Eighth Wonder of the World—our architect, who fell from the Memorial Church. Everyone was shouting and complaining, each in their own language, that they were not getting their fair turn. And then, believe it or not, a terrible thought shot through Alexander's head: that everything could sink into general chaos and even violence against those who had not yet been allowed to speak . . .

This fit of weakness undermined his worldly humanism. Must he make a feeble compromise? He had to find a solution, one as fast as the thought that had passed through his concussed head.

Suddenly the commander of the UN Peacekeepers, a general of African descent, was standing beside him. Alexander was not in the least surprised and, even more astonishingly, he found the strength to address him with the urgent request:

"General, please! None of these representatives of the international community should have to experience the slightest violence. I cannot tolerate it at the inauguration of the Eighth Wonder of the World in Macedonia. Remember, people have been waiting for this miracle for centuries!"

The commander of the Peacekeepers nodded at first, then answered with a rather unhelpful remark:

"Mr. Architect, Sir, I was just sent as an observer and am

not responsible for instituting order!"

"General!" Fallen Alexander shouted with such force that the Macedonian mountains trembled, the marble columns shook, and even the cradle rocked faster. "I'm not asking you to introduce order militarily, but I very much expect you'll be able to stick to simple alphabetical order!"

The general looked at him, bewildered. Alexander continued:

"The representatives of all 193 member states of the United Nations, large or small, must please be patient: we're following strict alphabetical order. The same applies to all unrecognized peoples who do not yet have a state, as well as to the many individuals who have come from all over the world: please be patient, everyone will have their turn!"

The general climbed the column that Alexander's father had come down, turned on the sound system, and began calling on those present at the inauguration to speak in alphabetical order.

"I ask the representative of Afghanistan to come up . . . Does Afghanistan welcome the establishment of the Cradle of the World?"

"Yes!"

"Does it welcome the utopia of cradlism?"

"Yes!"

"Has it brought a list of Savior Children and Murderer Children?"

"Yes."

"Let's go on: does Albania welcome the establishment of

the Cradle of the World?"

"Yes!"

"Does it welcome the utopia of cradlism?"

"Yes!"

"Has it brought a list of Savior Children and Murderer Children?"

"Yes!"

"Has it brought a lullaby that will be reproduced by the sound system of the Eighth Wonder of the World?"

"Yes!"

"Does Algeria welcome the establishment of the Cradle of the World?"

"Yes!"

"Does it welcome the utopia of cradlism?"

"Yes!"

"Has it brought a list of Savior Children and Murderer Children?"

"Yes! I'm so glad this has worked out."

"Has it brought a lullaby that will be reproduced by the sound system of the Eighth Wonder of the World?"

"Yes!"

"Does Andorra welcome the establishment of the Cradle of the World?"

"Yes!"

"Does it welcome the utopia of cradlism?"

"Yes!"

"Has it brought a list of Savior Children and Murderer Children?"

"Yes! It all worked like a charm!"

"Let's continue: does Angola welcome the establishment of the Cradle of the World?"

"Yes!"

"Does it welcome the utopia of cradlism?"

"Yes!"

"Has it brought a list of Savior Children and Murderer Children?"

"Yes!"

And so on. The general of the UN Peacekeepers read out the names of the states in alphabetical order, from A to B, C, D, E, F, G, H, I, J, K, L, M, N, O, P, Q, R, S, T, and U— but when it was the turn of the United States of America, a terrible silence fell. Only the waves of Lake Ohrid and Lake Prespa could be heard lapping the shore on both sides of the Galichitsa Range. All the ghosts and shadows, all the guests in his dream, all the living and dead who had come to express their support, turned into an ear—one single, universal ear that waited with trepidation to hear the representative of the land that had risen to become world leader and policeman after the fall of the Iron Curtain. And now, indeed, the envoy of the United States climbed the column to where the ceremony was taking place. He asked the general for permission to speak and addressed himself to the fallen man.

"Dear Alexander, dear Macedonian hosts, ladies and gentlemen from different latitudes and longitudes of our common home earth, it is a great pleasure for me to greet you on behalf of the Library of Congress in Washington, which tonight has particular reason to be proud of its holdings, where the greatest part of the memory, the knowledge, and the future of the world is preserved!"

The silence deepened. The Eighth Wonder of the World shone in the Macedonian night, all the 1,200 species of moths whirred in the air, all flora and fauna trembled with life (Macedonia being a superpower of plant species and moths), the columns swayed in a marble symphony, pointing toward the heavens, and the cradle rocked on its steel wires in an idyllic equilibrium in the grand holistic vision of its inventor, who had fallen from a great height.

The gentleman from America, a tall, middle-aged man with graying reddish hair, dressed in a black tailcoat as if for a reception at the White House, continued his speech:

"What reason does the Library of Congress in Washington have to be proud, you may ask?"

The silence was now of marble. Everything had turned to stone: the people, the living and dead creatures, the UN Peacekeepers, and the general of African descent. The fallen architect Alexander Simsar ran his fingers through the hair of his troubled head, and the participants from all corners of the globe heard that sound and felt that touch as if he was running his fingers over *their* different-colored heads. The speaker answered his own rhetorical question:

"The Library of Congress in Washington is the only institution in the world to ever own a copy of the five architectural projects of our dear Alexander, which we keep under the heading 'The Great.' The Library of Congress has the complete documentation, including the drafts, drawings, explanations, mathematical and static calculations, as well as passing philosophical comments on the five projects. These are, firstly, the All-Balkan Church of Love; secondly, The Death of Europe; thirdly, the tower of human bones named The Crimes of the Twentieth Century; fourthly, the International House of Global Poverty; and fifthly, the Museum of Political Lies from Antiquity to the Present.

"Yes, ladies and gentlemen, the Eighth Wonder of the World has been built by an author in the Library of Congress in Washington, whose talents were discovered way back in 1978. Thereupon he was closely observed on all the highways and byways of his émigré life and destiny—including the moment of his fall and the purchase of the complete medical records from which future generations of the international community will gain new insights. The documents also contain a detailed overview of the flora and fauna of Macedonia that was found in his apartment in Berlin-Kreuzberg, in a folder with the handwritten heading 'Macedonian Paradise.' It gives the Latin and Macedonian names of all the endemic species that exist only here and nowhere else, divided into a botanical and a zoological list. The former encompasses algae, mosses, and ferns, as well as the angiosperm dicotyledons and monocotyledons; there is a special overview of the woody species of the Galichitsa Range, of which we highlight the species underlined by the author: the alpine juniper, *Juniperus nana*, the Greek juniper, *Juniperus excelsa*, the Macedonian oak, *Quercus macedonica*, the wild cherry, *Cerasus avium*, and the European spindle, *Euonymus europaeus*. He gave particular attention to the variety of hackberry, *Celtis glabrata*, which exists only in Macedonia and the Caucasus. This is quite a mystery for the Pentagon research team that examines the geostrategic position and ecological singularity of regions thousands of miles apart. As far as the zoological part is concerned, there are 419 phyla of invertebrates and twenty-four of vertebrates, of which twenty are fishes. However, the most elaborate part is the one about butterflies and moths in Macedonia, with a special overview of the 1,200 Macedonian and scientific Latin names, although our team of entomologists has established that there are not 1,200, but actually 1,069 species. (Some exaggeration was involved and a few imaginary moths added.) I will take the liberty, dear Alexander, of reading out a few more names of these Macedonian jewels of nature because you have written remarkable things in the margins:

"In Macedonia, people have believed for centuries that every moth that flies up into the night sky is a human soul— the souls of all the nameless and innocent victims who have been killed throughout history, throughout the world. If we estimate how long the human race has already existed and how many millions of people have been killed for absolutely no reason, and then multiply the 1,200 moths by the number of days, and thus the number of nights per year, which is 365 (or 366 in a leap year), we arrive at 438,000 dead souls annually, who fly up into eternity.

"You write in this regard, dear Alexander: 'In a world with such a huge number of military bases, Macedonia is the only spiritual base, where aircraft carriers have been replaced by carriers of dead souls—the millions or even billions of souls in the memory of the world!'

"If for no other reason, Macedonia must be saved by the international community because of its butterflies! I'll begin with the names of the butterflies and owlet moths *Lepidoptera, Rhopalocera, Hesperiidae,* and *Noctuidae* in Latin, because this is an international gathering: *Zerynthia polyxena macedonica, Parnassius apollo macedonicus, Pseudophilotes bavius macedonica, Hadena clara macedonica, Acrolepia macedonica, Coleophora macedonica, Neurothaumasia macedonica, Rebelia macedonica, Zygaena achilleae macedonica . . .*"

The US representative read out the names of the Macedonian butterflies with such meticulousness and enthusiasm—as if they were nuclear warheads or something even more explosive—and the silence was so complete, that the ensuing protest of the commander of African descent of the UN Peacekeepers came as a liberation to the other delegates at the inauguration of the Eighth Wonder of the World:

"Stop this butterfly business!" the general thundered. "Does the USA accept the establishment of the Cradle of the World or not?"

"Yes! We not only support the Eighth Wonder of the World as an idea but also document and highlight the individual stages in the development of the architectural thought behind it. We also accept the utopia of cradlism—it sounds quite respectable in English—because we believe "there is no greater wealth and power on earth than man. We have also brought a list of the

Murderer Children and Savior Children to be carved into the columns of this edifice unique in the history of the world!"

Fallen Alexander Simsar finally took his hands out of the hair on his humanistic head. The representative of the Library of Congress continued:

"We also bring a lullaby composed by Benny Goodman, one of the world's greatest jazz musicians, who was inspired by the Macedonian diaspora in North America and created an immortal piece of music in the 1950s titled *Macedonia Lullaby.*"

At these words, the representative of the Library of Congress could no longer control the emotions bubbling up inside him and his tears began to flow. He cried like a child and couldn't pull himself together. He began to sway on top of the column, exactly 53.5 meters high—the same as the Memorial Church in Berlin, from which our hero had fallen. And Alexander thought: *Heaven forbid that he fall! That would be an international scandal with incalculable consequences for the future of the Eighth Wonder of the World and perhaps even for Macedonia itself! Many international historians describe Macedonia in particular as "the crossroads of dead empires" because the empire of Alexander the Great fell here; so did the Roman Empire, Byzantium, the Ottoman Empire, and the Austro-Hungarian Empire.*

The delegations, the Peacekeepers, and everyone present at the solemn inauguration stared mesmerized at the top of the column where the custom of "roof shouting" was taking place. Everyone looked up and thought: how can human tears cause a mighty construction to totter so much that it could topple down and bury us all? Was it going to collapse? How terrible! The American teetered and cried, as if his dearest person on earth had died. Oh my God, is the building about to collapse? No . . . yes . . . no . . .

Thousands of thoughts swept through the mind of fallen Alexander Simsar, too many to be recorded, but first and foremost must have been that he had never entrusted his designs to anybody; now it turned out that Washington knew everything about him. That is what he thought while he looked up at the American who kept tottering and blubbering. The whole of human history is actually the story of the fall, our hero thought: one by one, the empires fell here—real colossal structures, not just one human being, a drop in the ocean, or a grain of sand in the desert.

But this was the moment when the unpredictable saved beauty, in whose name the Eighth Wonder of the World was built, beauty for the whole world, our entire home on planet earth, and for all the people on it. Because the envoy of the Library of Congress had a small black suitcase with him up on the column. All at once he stood still, held onto the pillar with both hands for a moment, and then knelt and picked up the case at his feet; he took out a clarinet, which like the five-sectioned marble columns of the Eighth Wonder of the World consisted of three parts, fit them together, moistened the reed, and began playing Benny Goodman's *Macedonia Lullaby*.

Lo and behold, the strains of the song made the boat of Salonikan cherry rock, and all the 365 columns, all the steel wires and all the moths joined in to celebrate the victory of a nameless Macedonian architect and the proof that "there is no greater wealth and power on earth than man."

The mountains, lakes, and trees in the Macedonian forests sang; the stars, insects, and plants sang too, and even the fish in the lakes, while one lullaby after another, the songs of all the delegations, were sung as if by some multicultural jukebox; the commander of the Peacekeepers now identified completely with his role, enacted the alphabetical order with feeling and celebrated the first international consensus on a utopia—the utopia of cradlism, greeted with general acclaim!

The moment was so indescribably harmonious that fallen Alexander Simsar did not trust his own eyes and ears, nor his own Eighth Wonder of the World.

He stood up, raised his hands to the sky, and called his wife, his eternal love, to come and give birth on the summit of the Galichitsa Range, so that the first child to be rocked in the Cradle of the World would be their own.

"Come, my love! Come, you thoroughbred mother, like the first Neolithic figurines discovered in Macedonia thousands of years ago! Come, sun goddess, and bear me offspring!"

But it was not the sun goddess who appeared and stood before him, but Satanael Devil Shaitan Teufel Hudich Diabolus Gubernator Mundi.

"Excuse me, Mr. Satanael, did you happen to see my wife on the way here?"

"I saw her."

"Is she coming?"

"Yes, she's coming."

"And when will she be here?"

"The day hell freezes over!"

"What?"

"What do you mean *what*?! Have I not told you twice already, categorically, to get the idea of the new world utopia out of your concussed, sick head?"

"It *is* out of my head because I've now built the Eighth Wonder of the World—the Cradle of the World—and this act was greeted with international acclaim; a general of the UN Peacekeepers took over the inauguration personally, calling up state by state and people by people, you could almost say person by person. My architectural vision for this building also comes from the fact that I'm a philanthropist. Don't you see?"

"Now listen carefully to what I have to say. This is this third and final warning, otherwise you'll pay the capital price. The type of perspective on man's presence on earth that your so-called Eighth Wonder of the World or Cradle of the World opens up could have fatal consequences for the 'pale-faced biped' in all his multicolored versions. It could bring about the complete annihilation of the human race so dear to you! You've learned German—so just read Schopenhauer and you'll see what he writes. Basically he says: as long as intellect exists, it believes it only does good for the individual, but its nature creates a pure illusion that turns into an instinct: what is good for him is also good for the whole of humanity. In this sense, life is an eternally recurrent lie, not a gift but a culpable mistake in the double sense of the German word *Schuld*. Life is a process that is essentially incapable of covering its own costs . . . Are you listening to me, you fallen jerk? Have you ever looked up in a German dictionary what the word *Schuld* really means, and started to repeat: *Schuld, Schuld, Schuld*?!"

"Excuse me, Mr. Satanael, I asked you a moment ago about my wife. Did you see a woman on the way here, because she —"

"What woman, damn it? I'm telling you about a simple demographic law that every creature on earth should understand! At the beginning of the new era in the time of Christ . . ."

"Oh, Mr. Satanael, I'm to greet you from Jesus Christ. I met him briefly the day before yesterday and . . ."

"Don't interrupt! Where was I?...At that time, the total world population was around 250 million. It took a full 1,500 years—to the end of the fifteenth century in the great age of discovery—for that number to double to some 500 million. Let us continue: the billionth person was born only in the late eighteenth or early nineteenth century . . ."

"And greetings to you from Mohammed, Mr. Satanael, whom I also met . . ."

"Quiet! The second billion was recorded around the year 1930, the third in 1960 . . ."

"Mr. Satanael, Buddha also sends his regards. He came here and told me . . ."

"Hold your tongue, insect! The fourth billion was here in 1977, the fifth in 1988, just eleven years later . . ."

"And I mustn't forget Shiva and Vishnu-Krishna, nor the many Taoists who also greet you. You know, Mr. Satanael . . ."

"If one more word passes your lips, I'll strike you dead

on the spot! As I was saying, today we already have six billion people on the planet, and in less than thirty years we'll be nine billion. If humanity goes on this way, it will lead to complete self-annihilation of the human race by 2400. Get it into your thick head!"

The builder of the Eighth Wonder of the World was silent. Gubernator Mundi continued:

"Today's world is like a juggernaut heading straight toward three ominous icebergs. The first is the atomic iceberg—around thirty countries will have nuclear weapons within the next twenty years, and no one will be able to prevent their use. The second is the ecological iceberg: the huge power plants around the world, with their enormous carbon dioxide emissions, could cause disaster on a global scale in less than ten years. The third and final threat is the social iceberg, which is closely linked to economic crises and bank failures, and in thirty years' time will leave three billion people without the essentials of life—they'll be locked deep in the hull of the World Ship. Consequently, if one thinks rationally and proceeds from simple mathematics, as the White Trade International and the New World Order do in their analyses, one can get on with the extermination of half of humanity, or three billion people!"

In defiance of this threat, fallen Alexander Simsar protested loudly against the conclusions of Satanael Devil Shaitan Teufel Hudich Diabolus Gubernator Mundi:

"Mr. Gubernator, you can't do that! I'm expecting my wife, and she's about to give birth. We've been looking forward to this child for years. Please, even if it's nine billion . . . please let it be nine billion and one. Have pity on us. Do what you can to make it one child more. Have a heart, Mr. Satanael—there's nothing more beautiful in the world than the laughter of a child."

At these words, Gubernator Mundi burst into such laughter that the whole ship of the earth shook violently, both on the upper decks where some live in opulence and choke on it, and deep down in the hull, where people die in misery and despair—not only three billion of the living, but also three billion as yet unborn children. Gubernator's thunderous laughter made Alexander think perhaps he should not have spoken those last, elegiac words. *You fallen fool, you sure botched that up*, he said to himself. But Gubernator roared with laughter, took off his black glasses, and tore at his white hair and white eyebrows, and all at once everything about him started to distort: his white eyes turned to white pits, his white teeth grew into white marble columns, his white tongue turned into a marble-white cradle, his hair began to wave and to replace the steel wires that connected the cradle with the columns of the Eighth Wonder of the World. *No, I shouldn't have said those last, fatal words*, our hero thought. *Why did I do that? What the hell came over me? The white devil told me to be quiet!*

Now the laughter spread from the white mouth of Satanael Devil Shaitan Teufel Hudich Diabolus Gubernator Mundi to the lips of all the guests of the opening ceremony of the Eighth Wonder of the World, the "roof shouting" in the Galichitsa Range. Teeth gleamed in the smiling mouth of every single person present, beginning with the African general, the head of the UN Peacekeepers; all his soldiers laughed too, all the delegations to the last man and woman, and every person for themselves. Alexander wondered at the strange miracle his sick mind had produced, and he was amazed that neither military nor alphabetical order had been introduced. Rather, the human faces created an International confusion of laughter—the last International of the visible world—and they turned into an International of wide-open mouths that brought forth peals of laughter, and Alexander thought he heard the first verse of the true *Internationale*:

> *Arise, ye prisoners of starvation,*
> *Arise, ye wretched of the earth!*
> *(. . .)*
> *'Tis the final conflict,*
> *Let each stand in his place.*
> *The international working class*
> Shall be the human race!

In this rhythm that had turned to laughter, all the delegations that had traveled to Macedonia on paths unknown to him now passed before his eyes, each represented by their chiefs, all of whom were laughing in their own way. Fallen Alexander Simsar recognized differences in faces and intonation, although everyone was laughing to the rhythm of the *Internationale*. He was taken aback, for example, by the laughter of the head of the Chinese delegation, and it made him think that China felt threatened by little Macedonia that was using this peculiar construction, or the idea of such a construction, to try and rise above China as a demographic superpower. How could the Macedonian people, not only small and semi-recognized but also petering toward extinction, be about to build an eighth wonder of the world in the face of a people or alliance of peoples that had increased its population by one billion in less than fifty years? Our fallen hero felt terrible, if not mortally offended, and wanted to tell the head of the Chinese delegation: *Listen here, Sir, don't take my idea so literally and don't scoff at it. Haven't we just reached a consensus among all the representatives of the United Nations here and all members of the Security Council besides? They must comprehend an undisputed truth: 2,336 years ago, in the time of Alexander the Great, Macedonia was a great empire that stretched all the way to China. But what are 2,336 years compared with eternity? When we all met, I informed you that Lake Ohrid, which you can see from this mountain, is 150 million years old. So let's leave it at that; it's true that Macedonia is now nothing, but 2,336 years ago it was everything!*

Don't forget, the fallen man wanted to elaborate, *that Alexander the Great also had a linguistic vision: that Koine become the language of the whole world. And I ask you, would we be at any disadvantage if all of us on the planet spoke Koine today? That means that, if there are now 6,000 languages, that's 5,999 too many! If Koine had survived, there would be only one language and we could communicate like human beings, not like this . . . I don't deserve such unworthy treatment, Mr. Chinese Delegate!*

Such a pandemonium of laughter ensued that all the lists of Murderer Children and Savior Children that the delegations had brought to Macedonia for the Eighth Wonder of the World fell to the ground before his feet. The names were meant to be carved into the marble columns to put an end to bloodshed in human history, but now all the children began laughing, one after another, to the rhythm of the *Internationale*. Our hero felt they were countless children's heads, though not quite childlike but more like those of wizened children with wrinkles on their different-hued faces; and a different kind of laughter, which he associated with all the languages he heard at the topping-out ceremony, grew louder and louder with every passing second in his sick mind, concussed since the Memorial Church in Berlin, so that every sound of the International of Laughter that struck his injured brain center posed a dire riddle. Torrents of laughter turned into small white stones and pounded down on his head, and he began to count the aged children's faces that had turned into white stone: one, two, three, one hundred, 500, 2,000; he connected the different tonal nuances with the individual languages from the ceremony of gifts and lullabies; every white pebble was a language, and he took hit after hit in the same language, 6,000 times and more—in Shona, Swahili, and Bantu, in Bemba, Zulu, and Kurdish, in Lingala, Thai, Oromo and Pashto, Uighur, Tibetan, Tamil, Nepali . . . up to 6,000 times!

It was not a hail of words, but of song transformed into laughter; and not any old song, but the *Internationale*:

Arise, ye prisoners of starvation / Arise, ye wretched of the earth!

It was a universal deluge of laughter turned into little white stones; it was Koine, the universal language of the greatest emperor of all time, Alexander the Great. Everything laughed and taunted him all at once: the 6,000 or more Murderer Children and Savior Children, the 365 columns of the days and nights, the steel wires and the Salonikan cradle, the trees and the mountains, the plants and the birds flying overhead, and even all the 1,200 fluttering moths. And he said to himself in his jolted mind: *So all of you have come to Macedonia to laugh at my idea of the Eighth Wonder of the World; I thank you with all my heart. God's prophets Moses, Jesus, Mohammed, Buddha, Vishnu, Shiva, and the Taoists, are the only ones that have behaved humanely toward me. No one else has understood me other than my wife Tsveta, who will arrive at any moment to have our child. I ask myself here in front of you all what was my mistake and why do I have to reproach myself? I traced the paths of Macedonian alchemy in real buildings throughout the world, and my five ideas were pilfered straight from my MIND by agents of the Library of Congress in Washington; you have turned the only thing I accomplished into white stone—into sand, dust, and invisible air. Remember the dialogue between Emperor Alexander and his architect Dinocrates about the possible and the impossible. I'll now tell you the secret that was preserved on a parchment in the burned Library of Alexandria and was kept through the ages, until the twentieth century. If you don't believe me, I'll prove it with literary evidence. As an architect, I'm not very knowledgeable about literature, but may the earth's children whose books I've read come to my aid, those who were children and then died, one younger, the other older. May a girl come to my aid, who once frolicked through the meadows of Flanders and later wrote on Mount Desert Island, Marguerite Yourcenar, who names the alchemical principle of the Macedonian master builders: "Obscurum per obscurius, ignotum per ignotius" (The obscure by the more obscure, the unknown by the more unknown).*

Another child, living but elderly, Gabriel García Márquez, writes in One Hundred Years of Solitude *that alchemists came from Macedonia and created the Eighth Wonder of the World in Latin America then and there with a public performance (demostración pública de lo que él mismo llamaba la octava maravilla de los sabios alquimistas de Macedonia). Their leader, Melchíades, may have been a distant cousin of mine in that respect—blood is thicker than water. May another child come to my aid, one who was born a half-orphan in Algeria, the son of an illiterate Spaniard and an Alsatian soldier, and who later died when his car hit a roadside tree near Paris—Albert Camus, posthumously named "the last wonder of the Mediterranean," since he expressed in his unfinished books that "people die, and they are not happy"; so it is with my edifice, which cannot reward you with individual immortality, but at least with that of a collective kind. And may a child come to my aid, who was born in 1906 in Ireland under the name of Samuel Beckett, died in Paris in the late 1990s, was buried in Montparnasse Cemetery (Lot 8, Line 12), and discovered that "the sun shines on the nothing new" and "nothing is funnier than unhappiness."*

But no one came to his aid. The International of Laughter, like a Tower of Babel made up of cleft mouths, faces, and teeth of different colors, with outstretched tongues, went on in the rhythm of the stanzas that were translated in the twentieth century into all the world's existing and non-existent languages:

'Tis the final conflict,
Let each stand in his place.
The international working class
Shall be the human race!

For the last time, Alexander Simsar, the fallen master builder, raised his eyes to the sky, which God had drawn shut like a curtain so as not to see anything, and called out:

"Father, father, show yourself, come with your plumb bob and spirit level so we can see where I've made a mistake, because everything is raining down on my poor, concussed head. Why is this happening just to me, of all the unknown Macedonian craftsmen who built so many palaces and buildings around the world? Why is this happening now that I'm expecting my wife Tsveta to bear me our first child and save our Macedonian people from entering the annals of humanity with an empty cradle as its attribute?"

Then the sky, that closed curtain of God, opened a little, and he saw the head of his father Philip peer out. And, believe it or not, the head laughed together with all the other mouths of the centuries-old bloodline of the Simsar family of master builders, which was extinguished forever with his son. Our fallen hero asked almost soundlessly:

"Father, my father in heaven! Should your name be hallowed if even you laugh at me?"

He was left all alone. He could see nothing, neither heaven nor earth. The whole world disappeared—all of nature and the whole human race. Everything had turned to perfect white, and a great number of legends in various languages in the memory of the world, which lay about in the junk room of his jolted head, say that everything was white before the creation of the world, and that after the end of the world everything will be white again.

Now, dear reader, if you're still holding the pencil in your hand to participate in the construction of the Eighth Wonder of the World, which was born before it entered the head of the Macedonian émigré, architect, and facade artist Alexander Simsar, you can put it down. You won't need it anymore. The reason is simple: even in the sudden blindness that came over Alexander, he asked himself a question that was actually very rational: Why has nobody ever said what God did *before* He created the world? If it's true that everything was white before then and everything will be white afterwards, and if Satanael Devil Shaitan Teufel Hudich Diabolus Gubernator Mundi himself is white, you don't need to search long for the answer—it's obvious!

At that moment, in a flash, he saw white and looked into white; he felt a white breath blow into his face; a white hand with five white fingers ran over his forehead, and a white tongue with a white voice, which he recognized whitely, spoke to him:

"My fallen Simsar, thank you for the trust you've placed in me. I'd like to inform you most respectfully, indeed most affectionately, now at the very end of the third second of your respected fall: the willingness you've shown to cooperate thrills me most whitely! I'm almost bursting with white joy because you have only three tenths of a second left. You liberated yourself from the great malaise by the end of the third second and have recovered well, you survived the greatest malaise in human history, the incredibly nice-sounding humanism. Yes, by the end of the third second you realized there is no need at all for the birth of the next three billion basically innocent lives to be saved 'from the abyss' of the next thirty billion—or the 300 billion thereafter! They're actually 'non-existent subjects' whose limited lust for life will unavoidably be accompanied by threefold suffering.

"At the end of the third full second of your respected fall, which I by all means sympathize with, you've realized that all life is just a suspended death sentence—nothing but a white undertaking!

"I'd like to express my white gratitude for you having finally comprehended that it's all over!"

"What do you mean *all over*?" the fallen man asked whitely—white Alexander, invisible from whiteness. "How can it be all over if nothing has started? I'm expecting my wife, she's about to give birth to our child in the empty cradle. Please consider that we've been looking forward to this child all our lives. And so I whitely request, Mr. Satanael, I implore you, to please make a final, white effort! Where is she?"

The Envoy of the New World Order and the White Trade International, Satan Devil Shaitan Teufel Hudich Diabolus Gubernator Mundi, flew into a white frenzy and pronounced three dreadful white words. Even before the three tenths of a second had passed, which were left to Alexander as he was falling earthward, those words pierced his white, petrified, invisible, but still living heart:

"In heaven already!"

What happened then, you may ask yourself, dear white reader? Here is a white answer for you, divided into three white tenths of a second. Prepare yourself for the flight!

IN THE FIRST TENTH OF A SECOND, after the three full seconds of falling earthward, Alexander wanted to return and undo all he had done; and, sure enough, part of his wish came true, and he flew back up to the top of the Memorial Church in Berlin, and an idea of the Swedish mystic philosopher Emanuel Swedenborg he had learned by heart ran through his head, which had fallen but not hit the ground:

Marriage in heaven is a conjunction of two into one mind. It must first be explained what this conjunction is. The mind consists of two parts, one called the understanding and the other the will. When these two parts act as one they are called one mind. In heaven the husband acts the part called the understanding and the wife acts the part called the will. When this conjunction, which belongs to man's interiors, descends into the lower parts pertaining to the body, it is perceived and felt as love, and this love is marriage love. This shows that marriage love has its origin in the conjunction of two into one mind. This in heaven is called cohabitation; and the two are not called two but one. So in heaven a married pair is spoken of, not as two, but as one angel.

"The one angel is our unborn child and I must see it before

I die," fallen Alexander Simsar said to himself calmly and whitely as he rose up into the white endlessness, overcoming the double attraction of the earth, those 9.8 meters per square second, if we consider his weight of 67 kilograms (10½ stone) and height of 1.91 meters (six-feet-four); he reached the height again, at the top of the Memorial Church, from which he had fallen, exactly 53.5 meters above the ground, and called out as in the old Macedonian "roof shouting" custom, but now on the occasion of his own death: "I want to see my child and see my wife one last time!"

Exactly IN THE SECOND TENTH OF A SECOND, precisely at the height of 53.5 meters, at Berlin's 13 degrees, 24 minutes east of Greenwich, Satanael Devil Shaitan Teufel Hudich Diabolus was waiting for him and said:

"You once mentioned a parchment from the burnt Library of Alexandria that was built by the Macedonian dynasties— where they also erected the lighthouse, the Seventh Wonder of the World."

"That's right, I did mention it," fallen Alexander admitted, and even raised his voice unintentionally. "But I didn't want to endanger the Seventh Wonder of the World, by no means. Don't get me wrong, Mr. Satanael. The flame of the Seventh Wonder of the World burned at a height of 125 meters, and the ships and caravans that came from everywhere in the known world and brought the scents of Arabia, the spices of the Indian Ocean, and silks from all of Asia oriented themselves by that eternal flame; the eyes of China and India met the eyes of ancient Macedonians, Egyptians, Phoenicians, Jews,

Greeks, Persians, Arabs . . . The Lighthouse of Alexandria
was part of a kind of collective orientation and therefore 125
meters high . . . As for me and my idea of the Eighth Wonder
of the World, it came to me at the much lower elevation of
53.5 meters. If I had fallen from a lesser height I would have
made it lower because, unlike the collective orientation of the
Seventh Wonder of the World, with the Eighth Wonder of
the World I am proposing not a collective, but an individual
and yet international form of reconciliation, especially as the
peoples taken collectively, and individuals seen individually, are
not reconciled with each other and therefore produce death .
. . Since this idea came to me at the height of 53.5 meters, I
decided on this elevation, in all modesty, so to speak, because
I didn't want the construction of the Cradle of the World to
call the Seventh Wonder of the World into question. You must
agree, Mr. Satanael, that this idea popped into my essentially
worthless head 2,300 or so years later . . ."

At the same height of 53.5 meters, in that same second
tenth of a second, Satanael Devil Shaitan Teufel Hudich
Diabolus lost all control of himself and was at the end of his
tether:

"Stop blathering and tell me which parchment you mean!"

"It's one of the 700,000 papyri that were lost to fire when
the Library of Alexandria burned—the only one that was
later transferred to parchment in the period of Alexander's
successors," our modest master builder explained.

"Tell me in a nutshell what the parchment is about that you
so brutally diverted from antiquity's vast store of knowledge,

from which humankind has learned nothing in the centuries that followed," Satanael Devil Shaitan Teufel Hudich Diabolus Gubernator Mundi snarled.

"The parchment held the key of the universe through the centuries. The author of the mystery is Pythagoras, who formulated the principle 'All things are numbers.' Pythagoras is considered the founder of magical symbolism. The basic numbers $1 + 2 + 3 + 4$ are equal to 10. That is the key of the universe, arranged in the famous Tetractys of the Decad:"

$$* \\ ** \\ *** \\ ****$$

And there, at the height of 53.5 meters, at the top of the Memorial Church in Berlin, he drew these very points in the air for Satanael Devil Shaitan Teufel Hudich Diabolus Gubernator Mundi:

$$* \\ ** \\ *** \\ ****$$

He drew them in the air in the second tenth of a second and explained:

"The first is God, once and for all; the second is me, in my case—not because of me personally but because of my desire to build the Eighth Wonder of the World; the third is my wife Tsveta whom I'm waiting for and who is to bear our child; and the fourth is our unborn child. It's written on the parchment popularly called the 'key of the universe.'"

Satanael Devil Shaitan Teufel Hudich Diabolus Gubernator Mundi seized Alexander's right hand as it was drawing, at the top of the Memorial Church, and asked him:

"Do you know how parchment is made?"

"Yes . . . No, I'm not sure I remember," Alexander replied.

"Then I'll tell you so you know it for sure!" hissed Satanael Devil Shaitan Teufel Hudich Diabolus Gubernator Mundi. "Parchment is made by butchering a pregnant sheep a month before it gives birth. The lamb is taken from the womb, its skin is flayed, and everything that needs to be retained is inscribed on it with a red-hot needle! That's how it has been for thousands of years, and many crucial things in the memory of the world have been record in this way!"

Satanael Devil Shaitan Teufel Hudich Diabolus Gubernator Mundi held Alexander's right hand with which he had drawn the four Pythagorean numbers: the Lord, himself, his wife, and the unborn child. And as a legitimate envoy of the New World Order and the White Trade International, he quietly spoke the official message into Alexander's right ear.

"Firstly: God has drawn the sky shut like a curtain so

as not to see anything. Secondly: the master builder is at a height of 53.5 meters, from where he will immediately and unconditionally fall; his desire to create the Eighth Wonder of the World is nothing but a dull-witted, mortal fantasy, one of the millions, billions, and trillions of ideas born in as many human minds. Thirdly: the unborn child has been removed from the womb of his expectant wife, Tsveta. Fourthly: the unborn child's skin has been flayed, and the words have been inscribed with a red-hot needle: HUMANISM HAS NO CHANCE IN THE FUTURE OF HUMANITY!"

Satanael Devil Shaitan Teufel Hudich Diabolus Gubernator Mundi removed his white mouth from Alexander's right ear and, still holding his right hand, commanded:

"Open the fingers of your right hand in the air, Alexander Simsar!"

Our hero loosened his fingers, sure enough, and Gubernator Mundi gently slipped the parchment into his hand that for the first time in world history had been made of the skin of an unborn child—a long roll, as slender as a straw—and he clung to that straw at the top of the Memorial Church. In the second tenth of a second he looked up into the sky and reached for it with his left hand as well, and, like in the Apocalypse, the scroll began to slip away from him like a slender scroll, like a straw, like a delicate book, and he let his hands gradually fall toward the ground, following the parchment made of the skin of his unborn child, and that distance was exactly 53.5 meters . . .

IN THE THIRD TENTH OF A SECOND, his fall ended in a flash when his head hit the ground and he was killed instantly—on the stone sidewalk of Kurfürstendamm in front of the Memorial Church in Berlin.

So ended the idea of establishing the Eighth Wonder of the World, which has been in the minds of the Macedonian alchemists for over 2,300 years, because he, Alexander Simsar, knew that an idea that is not dangerous cannot be called an idea at all; he also knew that no utopia in human history lasting more than 3.3 seconds can be called utopia.

The Author

Jordan Plevnes was born in 1953 in Macedonia. He writes plays, novels, poetry, and essays, and his works have been translated into over fifty languages. His spiritual idealism is closely linked to the myth of the Balkans as the heart of Europe. Since 1988 he has lived in Paris, where he taught creative writing, and from 2000–2005, served as Ambassador of the Republic of Macedonia to France, Spain, Portugal, and UNESCO. Since 2007, he has been president of the private University of Audiovisual Arts - European Film Academy ESRA, Paris-Skopje-New York.

The Translator

Will Firth was born in 1965 in Newcastle, Australia. He studied German and Slavic languages in Canberra, Zagreb, and Moscow. Since 1991 he has been living in Berlin, Germany, where he works as a freelance translator of literature and the humanities. Firth translates from Russian, Macedonian, and all variants of Serbo-Croatian. His best-received translations of recent years have been Robert Perišić's *Our Man in Iraq*, Andrej Nikolaidis's *Till Kingdom Come*, and Faruk Šehić's *Quiet Flows the Una*.